## Brody Turned On His Heel, R

"Mr. Eden?"

"Yes?" He stopped.

Samantha rounded her desk and approached him. His body tensed involuntarily as she came closer. She reached up to the scarred side of his face, causing his lungs to seize in his chest. What was she doing?

"Your shirt..." Her voice drifted to a stop.

He felt her fingertips gently brush the puckered skin along his neck before straightening his shirt collar. The innocent touch sent a jolt of heat through his body. It was so simple, so unplanned, and yet it was the first time a woman had touched his scars.

Without thinking, he brought his hand up to grasp hers. Sam gasped softly at his sudden movement, but she didn't pull away when his fingers wrapped around her own. He was glad. He wasn't ready to let go.

His every nerve lit up with awareness, and he was pretty certain she felt it, too. Her dark brown eyes were wide as she looked at him, her moist lips parted seductively and begging for his kiss.

\* \* \*

***A Beauty Uncovered***
is a Secrets of Eden story:

Keeping their past buried isn't so easy
when love is on the line

\* \* \*

If you're on Twitter,
tell us what you think of Harlequin Desire!
#harlequindesire

Dear Reader,

While I was writing this book, the unthinkable happened. Nearly thirty people, mostly small children, were gunned down by a disturbed and dangerous man in Connecticut. Senseless violence happens more often than I would like to believe and I find myself at a loss about what to say or do when it does. This time, I was in the midst of writing a story about a man who'd survived his own brush with violence at the hands of his own father. It seemed like too much of a coincidence to ignore that Brody also grew up in Connecticut, less than fifty miles away from the site of the tragedy. So I decided to do something different this time.

At this point in the letter, I'm supposed to tell you all about how much you'll love this book and the characters. And I hope you will. Brody's story was the one I was the most excited to write and Sam is the perfect woman to draw him out of his self-imposed prison. But with everything that has happened, I'd like to tell you that this book is also about survival and perseverance. Brody lived through some terrible things in his childhood. Sam lost her mother suddenly and at a young age. I am sure that there would've been times when both characters thought the world was over and considered giving up. Life isn't always easy, but you have to hang on. Things will get better. Brody and Sam didn't give up, and in the end, they get their happy ending.

When this book comes out, it will be nearly a year after the Sandy Hook shooting. My thoughts are with the families as they face this grim anniversary and the holiday season without their loved ones. Things will never be the way they were. They will never get their children or wives or mothers back. I wish I could write a happy ending for them, too, but I can't. I can only hope that, in time, things will get better for them.

Please take the time to hug the important people in your life and tell them how much you love them. Also, consider making a donation to a charity that helps abused or abandoned children. Your kindness may be the very thing that gives a child the hope they need to make it through another day.

If you enjoy Brody and Sam's story, tell me by visiting my website at www.andrealaurence.com, like my fan page on Facebook, or follow me on Twitter.

Enjoy,

Andrea

# A BEAUTY
# UNCOVERED

—

## ANDREA LAURENCE

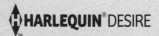

Recycling programs
for this product may
not exist in your area.

ISBN-13: 978-0-373-73272-2

A BEAUTY UNCOVERED

Copyright © 2013 by Andrea Laurence

**Printed in U.S.A.**

**Books by Andrea Laurence**

**Harlequin Desire**

*What Lies Beneath* #2152
*More Than He Expected* #2172
*\*Undeniable Demands* #2207
*A Very Exclusive Engagement* #2228
*\*A Beauty Uncovered* #2259

\*Secrets of Eden

Other titles by this author available in ebook format.

---

## ANDREA LAURENCE

is an award-winning contemporary romance author who has been a lover of books and writing stories since she learned to read. She always dreamed of seeing her work in print and is thrilled to be able to share her books with the world. A dedicated West Coast girl transplanted into the Deep South, she's working on her own "happily ever after" with her boyfriend and five fur-babies. You can contact Andrea at her website: www.andrealaurence.com.

To the Victims
of the Sandy Hook Elementary School Shooting—

This book is dedicated to the children who were lost, the teachers and faculty who died to protect them, and the families and students who will live with this senseless tragedy for their whole lives. My thoughts and prayers are with you.

# One

"Confidentiality agreement?"

Samantha Davis frowned at her godmother. Agnes had been there for Sam her entire life. She trusted the older woman, who had stepped in as a mother figure when Sam was still in elementary school. And she was helping her get a job when Sam needed it the most. But even then, she didn't like the sound of this.

Getting up to Agnes's office had been a feat of its own. Sam was pretty certain there were fewer security measures at CIA headquarters.

What was she getting herself into?

Agnes shook her head and pushed the form across the desk to her. "It's nothing to really worry about, honey. Mr. Eden is very particular about his privacy. That's why there are so many restrictive measures to get up to this floor. No one in the building has access except me, Mr. Eden and the head of security. I'm the only one at the company that ever has any personal interaction with him. If you're going to fill in while I'm on vacation, you will interact with him as well, so you'll have to sign the agreement."

An uneasy prickle ran up the length of Sam's neck. Although she and Agnes were the only people in the room, she felt like she was being watched. Looking curiously around the modern, yet comfortably decorated office, she spied a tiny video camera watching her from the corner. There was a second camera on the opposite wall to capture another angle of the room. Who needed surveillance equipment to monitor their secretary?

If it was anyone but her godmother telling her to take this job, she'd walk right out the door. But Agnes wouldn't rope her into a bad situation just so she could go on vacation for her fortieth anniversary. It must seem worse than it was.

And yet, she couldn't put her finger on what was really going on here. She scanned over the confidentiality paperwork with distrust. Brody Eden owned Eden Software Systems. Office solutions and communications. Nothing classified. Nothing that might threaten national security if it was leaked. And yet if she failed to follow the terms of the agreement, she would be obligated to pay a five-million-dollar settlement.

"I don't know about this. Five million dollars? I don't have that kind of money."

"You think I do?" Agnes laughed. "It's deliberately high to ensure no one breaks the agreement, that's all. As long as you do your job and don't talk about Mr. Eden to anyone but me, you'll be fine."

"I don't understand. Talk about what?" As far as Sam knew, Brody Eden was some kind of wizard behind the curtain. He was like Bill Gates without a face. Reporters had tried and failed to find information on him, raising even more questions, mystery and interest. He simply didn't exist before launching his software empire. If people found out she had access to him, she supposed they might come to her for details, but what was so important that she couldn't tell? How he liked his coffee?

Sam didn't understand all the mystery. She'd always assumed it was only to stir up buzz about the company, but the cameras and the contract made her wonder if there wasn't more to it.

Agnes sighed. "Sign the agreement and I'll tell you. It's not a big deal. Definitely not worth blowing this opportunity and this salary while I'm gone. You need the money. Sign." She pushed a pen to her and nodded. "Do it."

Sam did need the money. And the pay was very good. Too good. Suspiciously good. There had to be a reason why, but apparently she wouldn't know until she'd already signed her deal with the devil. Well, in the end, it really didn't matter. Her rent was due and she had fifteen dollars in her checking account. She picked up the pen, signing and dating the agreement at the bottom of the page.

"Excellent," Agnes said with a smile. "Mediterranean cruise, here I come." She got up from the chair and slipped all the paperwork in a folder. She carried it over to a small, silver door mounted in the wall that turned out to be some kind of drawer. Agnes placed the file inside and then slid it shut.

"What is that?"

"I was giving Mr. Eden your paperwork."

"You don't just walk into his office and hand it to him?"

Agnes chuckled. "No. I very rarely go in there."

Sam turned to look at the massive oak doors that separated them from the secret lair of Brody Eden. They looked like they would hold up to a battering ram and were likely wired with sophisticated locks and security like every other door she'd gone through. They were intimidating. Damn near unapproachable. And she was itching to find out what was on the other side.

"And he won't come out here to get it?"

"He does, but only when he feels like it. He communicates mostly through the speakerphone or the computer. He tends to email and instant message a lot throughout the day. The drawer works best for anything else. That's how you'll give him his mail and exchange paperwork with him. When he's done with something, he'll slide the drawer back to you."

"Like Hannibal Lecter?"

"Something like that," Agnes said. She sat back down at her desk, where Sam would be working for the next month, and folded her hands. "Okay, now that the legalities are handled, we have to have a chat."

Sam took a deep breath. The last half hour's discussion had built up a nervous tension that drew all her muscles tight. Now that she'd signed on the dotted line, she wasn't sure if she really wanted to know what was so closely guarded. And yet her curiosity was burning at her. "What have you gotten me into, Agnes?"

"Do you think I would've worked here for as long as I have if the job was terrible? I have had horrible bosses and he isn't one of them. I adore Brody like he's my own son. You've just got to learn how to handle him. He'll be less…prickly…if you do."

*Prickly.* Sam didn't like that word. She preferred her bosses to be without sharp, biting barbs. Of course, having a sexy, charismatic boss had only led her to heartache and unemployment. Maybe a prickly, distant one would be better. If she was rarely in the same room with him, she couldn't possibly have an affair and get fired.

Sam turned to one of the video cameras. She was uncomfortable having this discussion knowing he might be listening in. "Is he watching us on those?"

Agnes looked at the camera and shrugged. "Probably, but there's no sound. He can only hear us on the speakerphone unless you yell through the door. Right now, we're able to speak candidly, so I'll tell you the big secret. Mr. Eden was disfigured in an accident a long time ago. Part of his face was damaged very badly. He's very self-conscious about it and doesn't like anyone to see him. He also doesn't want anyone to know about his injury. That's the main reason for all the mystery. No one can know he's scarred like he is. When and if you do see him face-to-face, it's best if you go on like you don't even notice it. Keep the surprise, the disgust, the pity inside. It might be hard at first, but you'll get used to it."

She wasn't supposed to, but Sam couldn't help the pang of sympathy she felt for her new boss. How lonely it must be to live like that. It sounded horrible. It made her want to help him somehow. It was just her nature.

Her father had always called her "Daddy's Little Fixer." Sam's mother had died when she was in second grade, but being only seven hadn't stopped Sam from stepping up to be the lady of the house. She was never much of a nurturer, but she got things done. Socks with holes? Mended. No money for groceries? Macaroni Surprise for dinner.

If someone had a problem, going to Sam would guarantee it would get dealt with quickly and efficiently. Even if they didn't think they had a problem, she would fix it. That's why her two younger brothers referred to her as "The Meddler," instead.

But how could she help Mr. Eden if he kept himself hidden away? "Will I even see him? It sounds like he doesn't come out."

"Eventually, he will. Grumpy, like a hibernating bear. But his bark is worse than his bite. He's mostly harmless. Mostly."

Sam could only nod while she tried to absorb all of this. Agnes continued on, telling her about the various tasks she was responsible for. Aside from the basic secretarial stuff, she was also expected to run errands for him.

"I pick up his dry cleaning? Doesn't he have a wife or something to do that?" she asked as she looked over the list Agnes had typed up for her.

"No. He's single. When I say you and I are the only ones to see him, I mean it. You'll pick up coffee for him in the morning. Sometimes I get his lunch, but most times he will bring his own or have something delivered to the lobby, which you'll have to go get."

The man really didn't go out in public. It was mind-boggling. "How can someone live their life without going outside? Without going to the store or the movies or to dinner with friends?"

"Mr. Eden lives his life through his computer. Whatever he can do from there, he will. What he can't do, you do for him. You're more of a personal assistant than a secretary. He doesn't pay a premium salary for you to sit around filing your nails and answering the phone."

Apparently not. But Sam could deal with this. Now that all the secrets were out in the open, the nervous butterflies had faded. This might not be so bad. "When do I start?"

"Tomorrow. You'll shadow me tomorrow and Friday, and then you'll be on your own for the next four weeks."

"Okay. Any particular office dress?"

Agnes shrugged. "Most of the employees here are fairly casual dressers. Mr. Eden wears suits every day, although I've never been able to figure out why given no one sees him but me. You have such a flair for fashion, so I'm sure you'll be fine."

Sam tried not to laugh at her godmother's mention of her "flair for fashion." That was one way to put it. Another way was that she was obsessed with clothes and shoes. The more girly and feminine the better. She loved sparkles and glitter, pinks and purples. The right pair of platform heels or leather handbag could nearly send her into a climax.

Sadly, her past two months of unemployment had been devastating for her wardrobe. She'd gotten so discouraged from how everything ended at her last job that she'd slipped into wearing sweats and T-shirts all the time. Heels seemed like overkill for watching Lifetime movie marathons.

But that was in the past. She had a job, she was out in the world and her fashionable ways would reign once again. So yes, Mr. Eden would be getting a trendsetting eyeful from his little video cameras.

"Let's go get your badge and codes setup. They'll scan your fingerprint to get you access to this floor while we're there, too."

Sam got up from her seat and started following her godmother to the exit. Feeling brave, she stopped for a moment and looked back up at the video camera that was tracking her movements across the room.

Looking directly into the lens, she flipped her long blond curls over her shoulder and straightened her posture defiantly. "If you're going to spend the next month watching me from that little lens," she said, knowing he couldn't hear her, "I hope you like what you see."

"Like" was an understatement. Samantha Davis was distracting.

Brody had watched his new assistant train with Agnes for the past two days as though he were watching a fascinating new film. The two large screens that were connected to the surveillance cameras had captured his attention the moment Samantha came up for her interview. He'd ignored most of his work. Missed a conference call. He was just intrigued by her and the way she would turn to the cameras as though she were watching him as he was watching her.

He supposed it might be because he wasn't exposed to many people—women in particular—but even if he were, he couldn't help but think that Samantha would catch his eye. He liked the thick golden-blond curls that spilled over her shoulders and down her back. Her skin had a kiss of sun like she enjoyed jogging or swimming outside. He was drawn to her large brown eyes and bright smile. She wasn't particularly tall, but she made up for it with sky-high heels that made her legs look fantastic when she paired them with short pencil skirts.

She was really quite striking. Certainly a change of scenery from fifty-nine-year-old Agnes.

He loved Agnes like a mother. She was hardworking, efficient, if not a touch crotchety, but he liked her that way. Agnes was an office dynamo. It made Brody wonder how he was going to get through the next month without her.

Agnes had mentioned this anniversary trip months ago. He had had plenty of time to prepare. And yet, he still wasn't ready to deal with the actuality of her leaving for that long.

When Agnes suggested hiring her goddaughter to fill in while she was away, it seemed like a sensible suggestion. But he hadn't thought to ask if her goddaughter was attractive. He supposed most people wouldn't think that mattered either way, but it did to him. Brody avoided most people, but he avoided beautiful women the most diligently.

It didn't make much sense to anyone, especially his foster brothers, who were constantly riding him to get out and date. But they didn't understand what it was like. When they approached a beautiful girl, they only had to worry about rejection. And considering his three foster brothers were all handsome, successful and rich, they didn't get rejected very often.

When Brody approached a beautiful woman, he knew rejection was a given. But that wasn't the worst of it. It was the look on a woman's face when she saw him. That first reaction. That flicker of fear and disgust that even the most sensitive and polite person couldn't suppress. In Brody's world, that always came first, even if followed by a quick recovery and an attempt at indifference.

But what was even worse than that was the expression of pity that inevitably came. Brody knew there were people with worse injuries than his. Soldiers came home from the Middle East every day with burns that covered over half their bodies. They didn't hide away. Some were even outspoken advocates, role models for other victims. People were inspired by their strength to look beyond their scars.

That was a noble choice, but it didn't suit Brody. He hadn't been injured serving his country, and he wasn't interested in being the public face for acid burn victims. Being pitied one person at a time was bad enough. He couldn't take the massive public wave of sympathy all at once. He supposed that was why he'd gained a reputation of being not just a recluse, but a real bastard. He didn't like being that way, but it was a necessity. People didn't pity the villain, even if he was disfigured. They just figured he got what he deserved.

Turning back to the monitor that showed Samantha and Agnes going over some files, Brody sighed.

Looking at a beautiful woman, then having her look at you like you're some kind of sideshow freak... Brody didn't want to deal with that any more than he absolutely had to. And that was why he'd opted not to go out and introduce himself yet. Let her think he was rude. Everyone else did.

He was enjoying watching her from afar and not knowing what she looked like when she was horrified by his twisted and scarred face. She would be here for nearly a month, so Brody would probably go out eventually. But no matter how long he waited, she would still be beautiful and he would still be...what he was.

A loud ping from one of his computers distracted him from his dark thoughts. Spinning in his chair, he rolled over to one of the six machines that surrounded his desk.

The alert chimed after his web crawler software finished running one of its queries. He'd designed a system that scoured the internet daily for any searches or mentions of several things, including his given name, Brody Butler. The results were filtered to exclude any duplicates or mentions of the various Brody Butlers that he'd established as someone else.

From there, he'd review the results for anything questionable. Anything that might cause him or his foster family any grief. If someone, somewhere, was looking for him, Brody would be the first to know. He was a very private man, and he didn't want his past interfering with his present. It was the reason he'd taken his foster parents' name after high school. He wanted to put his childhood behind him. He wanted to start fresh and be a success because he was smart and savvy, not because people felt bad for him.

And for some reason, he worried that if someone connected Brody Butler and Brody Eden, it would lead to more questions about the past than he wanted to answer.

Blame it on his childhood, but Brody never let his guard down. If something could go wrong, he was fairly certain it would. His brothers accused him of being pessimistic, but he preferred to be prepared for the worst. He hadn't been able to stop his biological father from beating him, but he had always been mentally and physically ready when it came.

So, like he had as a child, he slept with one eye open, so to speak. His eye was on the internet. If someone was looking for him, the internet was the smartest place to start. And he would be watching and waiting for them.

"So what have we here?" Brody scanned over the report and breathed a sigh of relief. Someone named Brody Butler had driven his truck through a convenience store window in Wisconsin. False alarm. No one was looking for him today. Or yesterday. Or the past five years Brody had been watching. Perhaps no one ever would.

His former identity had vanished after he'd graduated from high school. He was simply another kid lost in the foster system. Not even his real parents had looked for him. His father had limited access in prison, but his mother had never tried to contact him, either. Given that she had chosen to side with her abusive husband over her scarred son, that was just as well.

Brody wasn't sure he would ever understand women. He was smart, caring and successful, but most women didn't see anything but the scars. And at the same time, his mother was attending every parole hearing, waiting for the day his abusive father was released from jail and they could be together again.

It was better he stay in seclusion, he decided. Women, beautiful or otherwise, meant nothing but trouble and pain. He was certain that his new assistant was no different. She was a novelty, a shiny new toy. It wouldn't take long before the shine would wear off and he could put his focus back on his work.

Dating the secretary was not only passé, it was a bad idea. Even fantasizing about it was certain to cause problems down the road. He'd be wise to keep his distance until Agnes returned.

Brody turned back to the surveillance monitors and found Samantha sitting alone at the desk. She looked so lovely with a blond curl falling across her forehead. It made him want to go out there, introduce himself and brush the hair from her face. It was a stupidly unproductive thought. He needed to stay as far from Samantha as he could. That meant working hard to put a sturdy barrier between them.

He pressed the button on the speakerphone. "Where is Agnes?" he asked.

His tone was a little sharp, and he'd deliberately skipped the pleasantries. He could tell she took offense to it by the way she straightened up at the desk and frowned at the phone. She brushed her curls over her shoulder with a sharp flick of her wrist and leaned in. "Good afternoon, Mr. Eden," she said in a pleasant voice, pointedly ignoring his question and emphasizing his lack of manners.

Interesting. Molly, his foster mother, would have his hide for being this rude, but he depended on his unpleasant reputation. It kept people away. Hopefully it would keep Samantha away, too. "Where is Agnes?" he repeated.

"She went downstairs to take a file to accounting and to pick up your lunch from the lobby. She left me here to watch the phones."

Lunch. He'd almost forgotten he'd ordered food from his favorite Thai restaurant. "When she comes back, tell her to bring my lunch in. I want to ask her something."

He watched her on the monitor as she considered her words for a moment before pressing the intercom button again. "You know, she's going to be gone for a month and you're pretty much stuck with me. Might as well start now. How about I bring in your lunch, introduce myself and you can ask me your question? I'm sure if I don't know the answer, I can find it out."

She was certainly a feisty one. Her second day on the job and she was already trying to push her way into his office. He was going to put off speaking to her face-to-face for as long as possible. Maybe even entirely, if he could.

"That won't be necessary, Miss Davis. Just send in Agnes when she returns."

There was very nearly steam coming out of her ears as she leaned in with a chipper "Yes, sir."

Brody watched for a few minutes as she angrily straightened up all the items on her desk. When that was done, she looked up at the camera. The breath caught in his lungs for a moment as he was pinned by her dark glare. He knew she couldn't see him, but it felt as though she really were looking right at him.

Looking at him without fear or pity or revulsion. She was irritated, yes, but he'd take that in a heartbeat to have a beautiful woman look him in the eye and not flinch.

Too bad it wouldn't be the same once there were no cameras between them.

# Two

"I need this job. I *need* this job. I need *this* job."

Sam pressed into her temples and repeated the mantra to herself every time Mr. Eden buzzed her desk, but it didn't do much to improve her mood. Frankly, it had given her a miserably pounding headache. It had only been three days without Agnes, but her godmother couldn't come back soon enough. She had the touch for dealing with the beast, but Sam obviously did not.

Agnes had warned her he was "prickly," and there couldn't be a more accurate description of him. He just rubbed her the wrong way. Okay, he was busy. He had an empire to run. But would it kill the guy to be friendly or at the very least, polite? To ask how her day was or to tell her good morning? But no, he only barked commands at her. "Get me this." "Go do that." "Pick up my lunch."

She'd already come to terms with the fact that she

was never getting into his office. He had shut down any suggestion she made that involved that, so the mystery would have to remain buried. But he hadn't come out of his office, either. He was there when she arrived and still working when she left. Why force her to sign a confidentiality agreement when the only gossip she could spread was that he was a jerk? From what she'd heard around the building from other ESS employees, that wasn't exactly a secret.

"I need this job."

Sam glanced at a few new emails and started typing up a letter. As the day wore on, it was getting harder to concentrate on her work. The headache was getting worse and she was starting to feel queasy. She hadn't had a full-blown migraine in a while, but if stress set one off, that's probably where she was headed. Her monitor was too bright. Every sound shot a sharp pain through her skull. She needed to go home, pop one of her migraine pills and take a nap to cut off the worst of it.

"Mr. Eden?" Sam pressed the speakerphone button, as much as she didn't want to.

"Yes?" His response, as usual, was impatient and short.

"I'm not feeling well. Do you mind if I go home?"

"Is it terminal?"

His blunt question startled her. "I don't think so."

"Is it contagious?"

Her new boss certainly had high standards for sick days. If she wasn't on her deathbed or in quarantine, he didn't seem to care. "No, sir. It's a migraine. My pain medicine is at home."

He didn't respond, but a moment later, the silver drawer shot out. Sam rose slowly from her chair and walked over. There was a lone bottle of ibuprofen in it. That wasn't quite going to cut it. Apparently Mr. Eden was not afflicted with migraines. But his answer was clear. No, she couldn't go home. She took the pills out and swallowed a couple. It was better than nothing. Maybe if she caught it before it was full-blown, she could keep it from getting too bad.

"I ordered Italian delivery for lunch," he said as though they hadn't had the previous discussion and the issue was resolved. "They should be in the lobby in about fifteen minutes."

It took everything she had not to reply, "And?" He didn't care that she didn't feel well. He didn't even bother to ask her to go get it for him, much less say "please" or "thank you." It was just implied. He never asked her if she wanted to order, either. If she felt better, she might want to smother her irritation with a layer of mozzarella cheese, but she was never given the option.

Sam couldn't quite figure out if he was some kind of genius who was thoughtless of others or if he just didn't consider her worthy of his attention.

"Put it through the drawer when it arrives," he added as though there were another option. He wasn't going to let her bring it to him, so in the drawer it had to go.

Without responding, Sam reached for her purse, pulled out a couple dollars and picked up the laundry bag he'd left by her desk that morning. If she wasn't going home, she might as well carry on as best she could. While she was downstairs, she'd drop off his dry cleaning and grab a turkey wrap from the deli next door. Maybe some caffeine would help. If she left now, she'd have enough time to run over and get back before the deliveryman arrived.

Her timing was perfect. As she strolled back into the

lobby, she saw the delivery guy at the desk with a sack of food. Sam grabbed it from him and headed through the ridiculous layers of security to get back to her desk. She set both sacks on the desk and then walked over to the minibar where Agnes stored supplies to get a cup for her drink. She was about halfway there when she heard his growling voice over the intercom.

"*Uh*...my lunch, Miss Davis?"

"One damn second," she said as she snatched a cup and slammed the cabinet door. She hadn't spoken through the speakerphone, but unless the walls of his office were made of soundproof material, he certainly heard her. She didn't care. Her head hurt, she was cranky and she'd reached her personal breaking point. There was no reason for him to be this rude.

Back at her desk, she clutched the paper sack with his food in her fist, ready to sling it in the drawer. Then she stopped. This whole thing had gotten old, quickly. He wasn't concerned about her headache, so she wasn't going to be concerned about his empty stomach. If he wanted food on his own timetable, maybe he should come get it. She brought it upstairs. He could come the last ten feet.

Sam slid the sack to the edge of her desk and looked up at the camera with an expectant arch of her brow. A moment later the metal drawer slid out to her. Nope, she thought.

She unplugged the cord from her phone, switched off her monitor and slipped out of her black Michael Kors cardigan. Walking to the closest camera, she whipped the sweater over her head, covering the lens. The other camera couldn't see her desk from its angle, so she returned to her seat and pulled her lunch out of the bag.

She needed this job, but *he* also needed *her*. If he

wanted his lunch, he was going to come out and get it. If he wanted her to do something, he was going to ask nicely. Sam wasn't working here to be abused. If he didn't like it, he could fire her, but she was pretty certain he wouldn't.

He had no one to interview a replacement.

Five minutes passed. She could hear instant messages chiming on her computer, but with the monitor off she couldn't see them. Another five minutes.

Then she heard it. The click of a lock and the turning of a doorknob. She'd roused the beast from its den. She was getting what she wanted.

And suddenly, she was nervous. She tried to go through everything in her mind that Agnes had told her. *Scarred...don't react...ignore it...* She braced herself for his appearance and her non-response.

The door flung open, and her stomach tightened into a knot. She expected him to charge angrily at her, but instead, she only saw his profile as he walked over to the surveillance camera and tugged down her sweater.

It must be the other side of him that was damaged because what she could see was...nice. Really nice. He was tall and strongly built, which was surprising for a computer geek. His expertly tailored navy suit stretched across wide shoulders. He had dark brown, almost black hair that was short but a little shaggy and curling at the collar. And his strong jawline, high cheekbones and sharp nose gave him quite a regal and aristocratic air.

He was actually quite an attractive man. He almost had a movie star quality about him. Sam preferred her men tall, dark and handsome, and he seemed to fit the bill. She didn't understand what he was...

Then he turned to face her. Sam struggled to hold a neutral expression as he walked to her, but it was hard.

The whole left side of his face was horribly scarred. The skin was puckered and twisted from his temple to his jaw and down his neck. It extended back to his ear, warping the cartilage and pushing his hairline back about an inch from where it was on the other side of his face. His eye, nose and mouth were unscathed, but as he reached out to hand her back her sweater, she saw why.

His left hand was scarred, as well. You could almost see the outline on his face where he had reached up to protect himself from something. She didn't know what, but it must have been horrible.

She swallowed hard and accepted her sweater, refusing to break eye contact. That part was easier because he had the most amazing blue eyes. They were dark blue like the most expensive sapphires, and they glittered just as brightly, fringed by thick black lashes. Sam could easily lose herself in those eyes and forget about everything else.

Only the loud click of the phone cord being plugged back in pulled her away. She looked down in time to see him snatch up his lunch. He paused for a moment, narrowing his eyes at her with a mix of irritation and confusion.

Unsure of what else to do, Sam smiled widely. She knew she was probably in trouble, but she'd used her brilliant smile on more than one occasion to smooth over her mistakes.

He didn't smile back. Instead, he turned and stomped back into his office without speaking. He slammed his office door so forcefully that Sam leaped in her seat.

And then…silence.

She kept waiting for a scolding from the speakerphone. An email telling her to pack up her things. Certainly she was due for a tongue-lashing via instant messaging at the very least. But it was silent in the office.

Maybe she did know how to handle him. Agnes certainly wasn't the kind of woman to take orders barked at her. Perhaps he needed to know what his boundaries were with her. His boundaries were abundantly clear and she'd respect them. For now.

Finally she was able to relax and eat her own lunch. Or at least she tried. A few bites into her wrap, the headache and nausea from earlier had faded, but something else seemed to be gnawing at her.

Her mind kept straying back to those beautiful, deep blue eyes.

Given the stern warning from Agnes about his face, Sam had expected him to be...ruined, somehow. But he wasn't. Yes, he was scarred terribly. It made her sick to her stomach to think of what he must've gone through to have scars like that. But that was only a part of him. The other side of his face was strikingly handsome. He was tall and muscular. She could easily imagine running her hands down the hard muscles of his arms and pressing her body against the wall of his chest.

And those eyes...

The tingle of anxiety from earlier had now become a tingle of another variety. Sam twitched uneasily in her seat and took a deep breath to wish away her misplaced desire.

"Enough of that," she said aloud. "We are not doing this again." Picking up her wrap, she took another bite and tried to force her mind onto her lunch and off of her boss.

If the fiasco of her last job taught her nothing else, it was that work relationships were bad. Relationships with your boss were catastrophic. Especially when they were married and conveniently left that fact out of every conversation they'd ever had.

Sam was naive when she had let herself fall for her boss, Luke. She'd let her guard down for the handsome, charming liar. But she'd learned a hard lesson she wasn't about to repeat. Given the circumstances of this job, she never thought it would be a problem. Brody was a grumpy, scarred recluse. Not exactly sexual fantasy material. But now she had seen him and things had changed. Which was frustratingly pointless. Agnes said Brody wasn't married, but he was as off-limits as any other employer.

Disgusted, Sam flopped her lunch back onto its wrapper. She needed to start focusing on work and maybe she'd forget about the whiff of his cologne and the full curve of his lips. Or not.

Maybe she should've just let him stay in his office.

Brody shouldn't have gone out there. He knew it, and yet he did it anyway.

Now he sat at his desk, silently brooding. He hadn't been able to touch his container of baked spaghetti for the past hour. It was his favorite, but he'd lost his appetite the minute he came face-to-face with Samantha Davis.

The surveillance cameras hadn't done her justice. She was absolutely breathtaking in person. She had a glow of confidence—a radiance—that didn't translate through the lens. Neither did her scent. Her sweater had left the smell of her floral perfume on his hands. When he got closer to her, he also picked up a hint of what he assumed was her cherry lip gloss. It had made her full pink lips shiny and alluring.

Brody was suddenly very warm. He kept his office

cool to offset the heat produced by all his computer equipment, but it wasn't enough. He leaned forward and shrugged out of his suit coat, tossing it aside. It barely helped.

He wanted to kiss her and taste those lips more than he had wanted to kiss another woman in his life. His body had quickly reacted to being so close to her. His pulse raced, his groin tightened and his grasp of the English language vanished. It was an instantaneous reaction. One that forced him back into his office before he made a fool of himself.

Samantha would never kiss him. At least not because she thought he was attractive and wanted to kiss him. On the one occasion in the past where a woman had appeared interested, it was his bank account, not his body that drew her in. Once she got what she came for, she was gone.

Truthfully, Brody had enough money for women to overlook the scars. He'd known women to put up with worse for access to the black American Express card. Every billionaire in Forbes magazine had some busty blonde twenty years younger than him clinging affectionately to his arm in photographs. It didn't matter how old or ugly or unpleasant the men were because they were rich. But that's not what Brody wanted.

He wanted more than arm candy or a trophy wife. He wanted more out of a relationship than what he could buy. He might get sex in a dark room. He might get companionship in exchange for expensive gifts. But Brody would never have love and he knew it. It only took one time getting burned to learn that lesson.

But Samantha gave him hope. She hadn't reacted the way he expected her to. There was the initial draw of air into her lungs, but there the reaction stopped. Or changed, he should say. Instead of her gaze running over his scars, it had found its focus in his eyes. There had been a softness there, a comfortable warmth in her dark brown eyes. And then...she had smiled.

No disgust. No pity. No irritation. If he didn't know better, he might think it was actually attraction. He'd seen the same look in a girl's eyes as she admired one of his brothers in high school. Or the way his foster mother, Molly, looked at Ken. But it had never been directed at him.

The problem now was figuring out what to do next. He was tempted to drop the rude act and actually try talking to her. Maybe from there he could consider asking her out. His gut warned him to stay away while his body urged him closer.

Turning back to the monitor, Brody lamented his inexperience with the fairer sex. The past few years with Agnes hadn't helped much. What if he was wrong about Samantha's reaction? He'd feel like a fool when she rejected him. And she would. The work relationship would be even more strained then. So he would keep his mouth shut on the subject.

But at least the worst was over. Samantha had seen him. The veil had been lifted and the awkward moment was behind them.

The chime of his email program turned his attention back to his computer. He had a teleconference with his executive staff in fifteen minutes. Not even his most trusted and senior employees ever spoke to Brody in person or saw his face. Typically his employees spent the entire time talking to a red curtain backdrop while he sat to the side. He could've just called a conference call, but he liked to see their faces during meetings. He could get so much more from their expressions than just their voices.

Before the meeting started, he needed the agenda and financial reports he's asked Samantha to pull together earlier.

Brody reached out to press the speaker button and hesitated. There was absolutely no reason to go out to Samantha's desk aside from the fact that he wanted to see her again. He almost wished she had recoiled in horror so he could return to focusing on his work instead of the sway of her hips as she walked.

Perhaps he'd read her reaction wrong. She might just have a good poker face. If he went out there and she avoided looking at him…if she shied away from his scarred hand…then he could return to his life in progress and know all was right with the world again. Yes, that was why he was going out there.

He pushed away from his desk and walked past the vintage pinball machine to the door. His hand rested on the knob for a few moments before he worked up the nerve to turn it. Earlier, he'd been angry and hadn't thought before he reacted. Now he couldn't shut his brain off long enough to make his wrist rotate. What if he was wrong? He didn't want to be wrong, but what would he do if she *was* attracted to him?

"Coward," he cursed at himself and forced his way into the reception area.

Samantha immediately shot to attention at her desk. She looked at him with wide-eyed surprise as he came out and approached her desk. Under the initial shock was a bit of apprehension. Her delicate brow furrowed as she fought a concerned frown. Was she afraid of him? She wouldn't be the first, although he hated to think so.

"Is s-something wrong, Mr. Eden?" Samantha leaped

up from her chair, nervously straightening her blouse and fidgeting with a ring on her right hand. "I apologize for earlier, sir. That was unprofessional of me. You'll come out of your office when you want to."

That explained it. She thought he was mad over her little stunt. She had probably been stewing at her desk, worrying she was about to get fired while he was thinking of kissing her. That only proved how far off base he was. He hadn't been thrilled at the time, but it was just as well that they got over that first hurdle. She wasn't about to be fired. Nor, sadly, was she about to be kissed. Brody shook his head dismissively. "No apology is necessary, Miss Davis."

She breathed a soft sigh of relief and every tense muscle in her body seemed to uncoil at his words. He couldn't help but notice every detail of her body from the slight movement of her full breasts as she breathed to the curve of her throat.

"Sam, please," she said, distracting him from surveying her body.

Sam. He liked that. There was something sassy and decidedly feminine about the nickname despite its traditionally masculine use. "I should've come out sooner. I'm very busy."

Sam nodded with understanding, but his excuse sounded lame to his own ears, so he figured it had to seem hollow to her, as well. "Of course." She reached down to a file on her desk and handed it to him with a wide smile. "Here's the report for your one o'clock meeting."

Brody froze in place, momentarily entranced by the stunning beauty of her smile. Full, pink lips. Dazzling white teeth. It seemed so sincere, begging him to trust her. It lit up her face, making her even more attractive.

His foster mother had always insisted that he was so handsome when he smiled. He never believed Molly—moms had to say things like that—but it was never a truer statement than with Sam.

He reached out and took the file from her, tucking it under his arm. At this point, he knew he should return to his office, but something kept him anchored to the spot. He wanted to stay. His mind raced for an excuse.

Brody sucked at small talk, so he wouldn't even try. Instead, he thrust his hand into his pants pocket and found his USB flash drive there. The tiny memory stick held most of his important files, and he carried it with him everywhere he went. It was perfect, he realized. Just the thing he needed to help him figure out if his new secretary was sincere or a really good actress.

Grasping the flash drive in his scarred hand, he reached out to her. "I need you to print a file off this drive while I'm in my meeting."

He watched as Sam looked down at the small device on the open palm of his hand. She hesitated for a moment and then reached out for it. Using her shapely, pink glittery fingernails, she plucked it from his hand without touching his skin. He might not have noticed how deliberate the movement was if he hadn't been watching for just such a thing.

Brody tried to swallow his disappointment. She didn't mind looking at him, but she didn't want to touch him. It wasn't surprising, but it was a letdown. She was polite and friendly to him because he was her boss. Nothing more. He should've known better than to let his mind wander to places it didn't need to be. "There's a white paper I've written on there about our latest database management innovations. Please print it out so I can redline changes later this afternoon."

"Yes, sir."

Brody turned on his heel, ready to return to his office and lick his wounds, when he heard her voice call out to him again.

"Mr. Eden?" she asked.

"Yes?" He stopped and turned back to her.

Sam rounded her desk and approached him. His body tensed involuntarily as she came closer. She reached up to the scarred side of his face, causing his lungs to seize in his chest. What was she doing?

"Your shirt…" Her voice drifted off.

He felt her fingertips gently brush the puckered skin along his neck before straightening his shirt collar. It must've flipped up when he took his suit coat off earlier. The innocent touch sent a jolt of heat through his body. It was so simple, so unplanned, and yet it was the first time a woman had touched his scars.

His foster mother had often kissed and patted his cheek, and nurses had applied medicine and bandages after various reconstructive procedures, but this was different. As a shiver ran down his spine, it *felt* different, as well.

Without thinking, he brought his hand up to grasp hers. Sam gasped softly at his sudden movement, but she didn't pull away when his scarred fingers wrapped around her own. He was glad. He wasn't ready to let go. The pleasurable surge that ran up his arm from her touch was electric. His every nerve lit up with awareness, and he was pretty certain she felt it, too. Her dark brown eyes were wide as she looked at him, her moist lips parted seductively and begging for his kiss.

He slowly drew her hand down, his eyes locked on hers. Sam swallowed hard and let her arm fall to her side when he finally let her go. "Much better," she said, gesturing to his collar with a nervous smile. She held up the flash drive in her other hand. "I'll get this printed for you, sir."

"Call me Brody," he said, finding his voice when the air finally moved in his lungs again. He might still be her boss, but suddenly he didn't want any formalities between them. He wanted her to say his name. He wanted to reach out and touch her again. But he wouldn't.

Sam looked away to glance down at the pink and crystal watch on her delicate wrist. Brody couldn't help but notice how every detail about her was so...*sparkly*. Her watch was simply the latest piece. The large cocktail ring on her right hand made her earrings look demure. The stitching on her silk blouse reflected the light as did the glitter that seemed to be embedded in her pink eye shadow. Her heels had a pattern of sequins and stones across the toe shaped like a daisy. Even the buttons on her sweater looked like dime-sized diamonds.

He wasn't used to that. His sister, Julianne, was feminine, but she was also raised in a house full of boys. She could hold her own and very rarely, if ever, sparkled. Most of the time, she was actually covered in sculpting mud from her pottery.

"You're going to be late for your executive meeting, Brody."

His name coming from her lips sounded wonderful to his ears, but he couldn't dwell on it. He looked down at his own watch, which was expensive, painstakingly accurate, but not at all flashy. She was right. He reluctantly took the file out from under his arm and held it up as he backed away. "Thanks."

Returning to the safety of his office, he closed the door and flopped his back against the solid wood. He took his first deep breath in five minutes, the scent of her perfume in his lungs. It made his head swim, the blood rushing from his extremities to fuel his desire with a restless ache he'd grown accustomed to over the years.

No woman, sparkly or otherwise, had ever deliberately touched his scars like that. With every fiber of his being, he wanted her to do it again.

# Three

The house was empty. It always was when Brody came home. At least as far as people were concerned. He hung his overcoat on the hook by the garage entrance, tossed his laptop bag onto the kitchen table and whistled loudly.

His answer came in the form of excited clicks of toenails on the hardwood floor and thumps down the stairs. A few moments later, a large golden retriever rounded the corner and bounded straight for him. Brody braced himself as the dog stood up onto her hind legs and placed her paws on his chest. Normally she met him at the door, so she must've been sound asleep on her giant beanbag pillow upstairs.

He leaned down to let her lick him and scratched gently behind her ears. "Hey there, Chris. Did you have a good day with Peggy?"

The dog jumped down and danced around his feet,

her tail wagging enthusiastically. Chris was a very happy dog and a great companion for Brody. It was impossible for him to sulk with her around. His foster sister, Julianne, had gotten the puppy for him as a birthday present three years ago. She decided that he needed a hot blonde in his life, so he named her after sexy pop singer Christina Aguilera as a joke.

Admittedly, she had been a great gift. She kept Brody company in his big empty house. His housekeeper, Peggy, walked and cared for her during the day, and the dog occasionally stayed with Agnes if Brody had to travel. It wasn't much of a burden. Everyone loved Chris.

"Did Peggy feed you dinner yet?"

Chris darted over to her empty bowl and stared up expectantly. Brody looked down into the dog's big brown eyes and knew she'd never admit it, even if she'd already eaten. She was a canine garbage disposal. "Here you go," he said, filling her bowl with her favorite kibble. "I wonder what Peggy left for me to eat?"

He had a good guess. Tonight, the air was filled with the spicy scent of Mexican food.

Peggy arrived after he left for work and was gone before he came home. She kept his place tidy, took care of Chris, handled the laundry that didn't go to the cleaners and did all his grocery shopping and cooking. Peggy was an excellent cook. She made a pot roast so good it could make you cry. It was even better than Molly's, although he wouldn't admit to that even if one of his brothers had him in a headlock.

Peggy had worked for him for five years, but Brody wasn't entirely sure what she looked like. There was a copy of her driver's license photo in her file from her background check, but few people actually looked like their pictures. Agnes had interviewed her, so he'd never met Peggy in person. All he knew was that she could deal with his idiosyncrasies, and that made her perfect.

Brody tossed his suit coat over the stool at the kitchen bar and looked for the note Peggy left him every night. He'd bought her nice stationery with an embossed "P" on the front and she'd opted to use it for her daily communications with him.

He found it sitting beside a plate of freshly baked chocolate chip cookies on the kitchen island. He popped one in his mouth and groaned. That woman deserved a raise. He chewed as he flipped open the card.

*There's enchilada casserole in the oven. Picked up your favorite beer at the store today. It's in the fridge. New sheets on the bed. Mail on your desk. Chris has eaten dinner, don't let her fool you. You also got a package from your brother.—Peggy*

A package from his brother? Frowning, Brody set down the card, went to the fridge for a bottle of microbrew and snatched up another cookie. He carried both of them down the hallway into his study with Chris quick on his heels. On his desk was a stack of various bills, junk mail and a large brown box. The label said it was from his foster brother Xander.

Brody had gone to live with Ken and Molly Eden when he was eleven, only a few months after his father had attacked him. He grew up on their Christmas tree farm in Connecticut with their daughter, Julianne, and a list of other foster children. He considered the Edens and the three other boys that remained on the farm— Wade, Xander and Heath—his true family. Xander and his younger brother, Heath, had come to the farm after their parents were both killed in a car accident. Xander was in the same grade as Brody, just a few months younger. He was currently a Connecticut congressman living in D.C.

He ignored the mail and went straight to the package. It wasn't his birthday. It was October and far too early for a Christmas present. There was no reason he should be getting a box from Xander, so it was a mystery. Until he ripped the brown paper away to reveal a picture of an inflatable woman.

The torture of brothers never ended. Neither miles nor years would get them off his back about his love life. He knew it would be even worse if they ever learned the truth of it. Brody dropped the box onto his desk and went for his phone.

"This is Langston," Xander answered.

"You know," Brody began, skipping the small talk. "I expect this kind of crap from Heath, but not you. You're supposed to be the sensible, non-controversial one."

"At the office, absolutely. But the rest of the time, I'm your brother and it is fully within my rights to give you grief about your love life, or lack thereof."

"You have no room to talk, Xander. When was the last time you actually went on a date?"

"I took Annabelle Hamilton to a reception last week."

Brody chuckled and sat back on the edge of his desk. "A political fund-raiser?"

"Well, yes, but—"

"Doesn't count. When was the last time you went on a date where you didn't talk about politics, attend a political event or leave your date stranded alone while you talked to some lobbyist that came up to your table?"

There was a long silence before his brother spoke. "I reject the unreasonable boundaries you've placed on my love life. The life of a single congressman is complicated." Xander said the words with his official man-in-power voice, as though he were addressing a congressional committee.

"That's what I thought. You should've kept that doll for yourself."

Xander laughed, turning from his phone to say something to someone else. Despite the late hour, he was still at the office. Xander was always at the office.

"Got someone with you?" Brody asked.

"One of my congressional interns. He's leaving for the night and reminding me about my early appointment tomorrow. I have to give some VIPs from my district a tour of the Capitol building."

Brody settled into the brown leather loveseat in his office. Chris immediately jumped up beside him, curling up to lie down with her head in his lap. His free hand went to rub her ears. "It's awfully late to still be at the office. I'd hate to work for you. You're a mean boss."

"Not as mean as you are. At least I speak face-to-face with my employees instead of barking at them over an intercom."

"I pay them well for the inconvenience of dealing with me," Brody argued.

"That's fair, I suppose. Mine don't get paid. It's the beauty of government internships. I can work their idealistic hearts to death for free so when they graduate college, they will be jaded and fully prepared for a job in public service."

"You sound run down, Xander. Are you sure you're up for a campaign and another term?"

"I've just had a long day. I don't have much free time. And I know that both of us aren't the best at making time to date. Which is why I sent that lovely plastic woman to you. It's secretly an invitation to a fund-raiser my party is having next week. If I sent you a card, I knew you'd ignore it, but that doll got you on the phone."

Of course. There was always something behind it. He would've ignored an invitation. And he'd ignore this one, too, after he hid it away where Peggy wouldn't find it and faint. "I'll mail a check."

"I don't want you to mail a check, Brody. I want you to come."

Oh, yeah, because socializing at a cocktail party with a bunch of strangers was his idea of a good time. He'd jump right on the next train from Boston. Xander knew it, too, so there had to be more to the story than he was telling. "What's her name?"

"Why would you—?"

"You're as transparent as Mom."

Xander sighed heavily into the phone receiver. "Her name is Briana Jessup. *Dr.* Briana Jessup. I met her a few weeks ago. She's a plastic surgeon that specializes in reconstructive surgery. She spends several weeks a year in third world countries helping disfigured children."

Brody listened to his brother talk, but the more words that came out of his mouth, the more irritated he got. "I don't know which is worse. Thinking you're fixing me up on a date again or trying to lure me to another doctor."

"It's just social," Xander corrected. "I thought you might be more comfortable with a woman if you knew she had…" His voice trailed away as though he weren't quite sure how to say it. Xander was always on a mission to find the right way to say things. It made him a great politician. But dealing with him as a brother could be frustrating when everything he said was polished to a point of near insincerity.

"Seen worse?" Brody suggested.

"You know what I mean, man. Don't get offended."

Brody took a sip of his beer. He understood what his brother was doing. It wasn't a bad idea. A woman who had experience with severe injuries like his might not react so negatively to it. She might even touch him, although it might be more for professional curiosity than attraction. It was certainly a better choice than the last woman Xander tried to set him up with. "I'm not offended. I'm just not interested in starting up something with this doctor of yours."

And he wasn't. Maybe if Xander had asked him a week ago. But now, his mind was overrun with thoughts of one particular woman touching him. A sunny blonde with luscious curves and an affinity for pink.

"Then are you still upset about the thing with Laura? It's been three years."

Brody chuckled into the phone. "Why would I still be upset about Laura? Just because you set me up with a woman that pretended to like me long enough to steal my personal information and charge a hundred-thousand dollars on my credit cards…? I mean, after three years that would be petty of me."

Xander sighed. "You know I'm sorry about that. She seemed like she really liked you, and I hate that she stole from you. But this other lady is different. I think you'd really like her."

"I'm too preoccupied for something like that right now. I have my mind on…other things."

"Are you seeing someone?" Xander asked, his voice laced with an edge of incredulity.

"No," Brody said. "Don't be ridiculous."

"But you're *interested* in someone, aren't you?"

That, Brody couldn't argue with. He was interested. He didn't know if that would make any difference in the end, but he was. He couldn't stop thinking about Sam and what it would feel like to touch her.

"I suppose you could say that...."

Sam slammed back another shot of espresso from the coffee shop in the lobby, but she wasn't sure it would help. The first four hadn't. She was still exhausted. She hadn't gotten much sleep last night. Her mind kept spinning with the previous day's developments.

She had started Wednesday irritated with her boss. Brody was demanding, rude and thoughtless of others. By the time she went home, she was intrigued by him. More than that—aroused by him. When she wasn't lying in bed fantasizing about touching him again, she was plagued with questions.

*What happened to him? How long had he been like that? How could he live his life separated from other people? Wasn't he lonely? Why was he so unpleasant?*

The "fix-it gene" in Sam was alight with the need to get her hands on Brody's life and put it right. It seemed a shame to her that he was hiding. He was a smart, successful and handsome man. He shouldn't let his accident keep him from living a full life.

Sam eyed the door to his office. She wanted to march in there, grab him by the hand and drag him out into the sunlight. It would be good for him, she was certain.

Then she saw it. The door was ever so slightly ajar. It hadn't quite latched earlier. That was odd. Brody was always very meticulous about shutting and locking the door. His mind must be on other things.

Or maybe it was a subtle invitation. A subconscious

slip. Sam wasn't a big believer in accidents. Everything happened for a reason. What if Brody wanted a fuller, more open life, but didn't know where to start? She could help him. Maybe he knew that. Could this be his way of reaching out?

"Sam, could you get me that new distribution proposal?" Brody's voice crackled over the speakerphone.

"Yes, sir."

Sam grabbed the file out of her inbox and let her gaze wander between the silver drawer and the unlatched door. She wasn't sure if Brody left it open on purpose, but she decided to take the opportunity fate, or Brody, had provided.

She quickly reached down for her purse and pulled out her compact. Her makeup was good. Her blond curls were swept back into a messy bun today. Her lip gloss was still shiny. She looked great.

Getting up from her seat, she tucked the file under her arm and gently tugged down at the hem of her sweater dress. She smoothed over her wide, patent leather belt before reaching out and grasping the doorknob. She didn't have to turn it. The light pressure was enough to unlatch it completely and the door swung open.

Sam poked her head into the dark room, expecting Brody to start yelling at her at any moment, but there was nothing. As her eyes adjusted, she noticed a pinball machine to her left. Beside it was a Track and Field arcade game. Both of them flashed and blinked, lighting the corner of the dim room. Beyond that, she spied a seating area with plush, leather couches. A small kitchenette with a sink and a refrigerator.

In the corner were a universal weights machine and a treadmill. That explained those arms. She half expected to see a bed, but that was the only thing missing. He had his own little world behind these doors.

Taking a step inside, she found his desk to the right. It was a large U-shaped configuration with multiple monitors and computers. The first two screens she looked at displayed the feed from the lobby surveillance cameras. He had a good view of her at her desk, despite the grainy black-and-white feed. He was currently facing the other direction or he would've seen her approach his door and come into his office space.

Sam took a deep breath and closed the gap between them in a few steps. The hum of the multiple computers and the constantly running air-conditioning unit disguised the click of her heels across the marble floor.

When she was about a foot behind him, Sam paused, looking down at a large bowl of multicolored jelly beans on his desk, giving a bright pop to an otherwise monochromatic space. Her bravery was waning. But it was too late to turn back. He'd likely notice her making a quick escape. Instead, she decided to wait a moment and see if he finally turned around. Saying his name would probably send him three feet out of his chair.

Sam's gaze drifted past his shoulder to the screen he was staring so intently at. At the top was the name "Tommy Wilder" with a long series of links and descriptions that were too small for her to read. She'd never heard of Tommy Wilder. Then she spied the screen beside it, where her own name was shown just as prominently. Was he doing some kind of background check on her?

She couldn't help the gasp that escaped her lips. She was close enough to Brody now that the small sound caused him to immediately spin in his chair to face her.

His initial look of surprise quickly morphed into

anger as his jaw locked and his eyes narrowed at her. He stood up in one fluid movement and Sam took an instinctive step backward.

"What the hell are you doing?" he asked. "How did you get in here?"

Sam clutched the file to her chest and took another step back as he charged forward. "I brought the file you w-wanted. The door was open and I—"

"What? You thought I left it open for *you?*" he interrupted her shaky explanation.

Apparently her ideas about Brody subconsciously reaching out to her were woefully incorrect. "No, I..." She didn't have a better explanation. She took another two steps back, pausing when she felt the press of cold metal on her back. A quick glance showed her she'd backed herself against the pinball machine. With Brody moving closer, she was pretty much trapped there to take her punishment.

"What did you see?" he asked, pointing to his computers. "Tell me," Brody demanded, his booming voice amplified by the acoustics of the dark room.

Sam was wide-eyed with confusion. He was mad that she was in there, but somehow he seemed more concerned that she was spying on him. What did she see? Nothing important. What did it matter, anyway? She had a confidentiality agreement in place. She could've seen the truth about the Roswell crash site and the JFK assassination and she couldn't tell anyone. "Just some names. My name. Nothing else."

Brody crowded into her space, placing his hands on each side of the pinball machine as though he were playing to prevent her escape. His blue eyes were nearly black in the dim lighting as he leaned into her.

Even with the file between them, Sam could feel the

heat of his body penetrating her clothes. The scent of his cologne crowded her, filling her lungs as she took a deep breath to calm herself.

Goodness, but he was tall. In her four-inch heels, she was almost looking him in the eye, their bodies aligning perfectly. Her heart started racing as she thought about reaching out and touching him. Her touch before had been fleeting, innocent, yet powerful. She craved that connection again. It was a ridiculously counterproductive thought, given the man was in a big enough rage to fire her, not kiss her.

Sam licked her lips, noting his gaze dropped down to watch, then came back up to look into her eyes. She had her share of experience with men, and she knew when a man wanted her. Sam was surprised, given all the barriers Brody had deliberately put between them, but it was clear. He wanted her. Yet he was holding back.

"What was the other name?" His voice was calmer now but still deadly cold.

Sam was so wrapped up in her thoughts about Brody that she could barely remember. "Timmy? Tommy? I don't know. I only saw it for a moment."

At that, Brody nodded and the muscles in his body seemed to uncoil from the pounce he'd been ready to make. But he didn't pull away. He stayed put.

The blinking lights of the pinball machine behind her cast Brody's face in dancing shadows. He was so beautiful, and yet, so damaged. She watched him, knowing she shouldn't linger too long on his injuries, but wanting to understand what he'd been through.

Before she could stop herself, she reached her right hand up and placed it on his damaged cheek. Her palm barely made contact with the wavy surface of his skin before he jerked back. Sam didn't want him to shy away. She wasn't afraid of him or his injury.

Slipping her hand behind his neck instead, she pulled him forward, meeting his lips with her own. His mouth was stiff against hers at first, making her fear she'd made a gross miscalculation in kissing him, but then he relaxed and she felt one of his hands move to her waist.

His lips were soft and slightly sweet, as though he'd been eating some of those jelly beans she'd spied on his desk. Like his office, he seemed to be just as physically closed off. Sam had to coax his mouth open wider, running her tongue along his bottom lip to let her in.

Sam anxiously waited for Brody to take charge of their kiss. To press her back against the pinball machine and dig his fingertips hungrily into her flesh. But he didn't. His every move was hesitant, as though he were thinking about it. You weren't supposed to think about a kiss, you were supposed to feel and give in to it.

The file she'd been holding slipped to the floor. Sam didn't care. With both hands free, she wrapped her arms around his neck, easing closer to him. If he wasn't going to do it, she would.

Her move made him bolder. He pressed into her, snaking his arms around her waist. She could feel every hard inch of him as he leaned in and she arched her body against him. The movement elicited a low groan against her lips.

The sound was a reality check for Sam. Even though she'd been the aggressor, it wasn't until that moment that she really realized what she'd been doing.

Kissing her boss. *Again.* She was determined to let history repeat itself. Last time was a disaster. Why would it be any different now?

Sam placed her hands against Brody's chest and gently pushed until their lips parted and he eased back. They stood still, their warm breath lingering in the space between them. Finally, she crouched down to gather up the paperwork she dropped and pressed the mess of the distribution proposal against his chest.

Brody took another step back, clutching the wild scattering of paper. But his eyes didn't leave hers. There was a curious expression there as he watched her. His eyes narrowed, confusion and distrust still evident, but eventually, that faded into confidence.

And then, for the first time, the corners of Brody's mouth curled upward and he smiled at her. Her knees started to quiver beneath her. His smile was so charming it caught her off guard. His whole face lit up, his eyes twinkling with a touch of mischief. It made him even more handsome, if she could believe it. His smile made her want to tell him stories to make him laugh. It made her want him all the more.

A hot flush swept over her body as the rush of arousal from their kiss surged through her with no outlet. Her fingertips tingled where she touched him and ached to reach for him again. Her heart was still racing, although the flash of his smile had caused a momentary skip in her chest.

This was bad. Very bad. She needed to get out of here before she completely lost her mind and started taking her clothes off.

Turning on her heel, Sam rounded the pinball machine and ran from Brody's office, slamming the door shut behind her.

# Four

Sam didn't say good-night when she left. Brody had simply looked up at his surveillance monitor at some point and noticed her desk was empty and her coat was gone. It was just as well. If she'd tried speaking to him, he doubted he would've managed a sensible response.

Even three hours later, the cacophony of thoughts in Brody's head made it hard for him to think. He'd gotten zero work done. There was no way he could focus properly. In a flash, so many things had gone right and wrong at once.

She'd kissed him. Really kissed him. It wasn't some chaste peck or tight-lipped obligation. It had fallen nearly into the "making out" category, by his assessment, such as it was. But she'd also snuck into his office, spied over his shoulder and completely invaded his personal space. It didn't really matter, though. Brody found he couldn't be mad at her while he could still taste that cherry gloss on his lips.

It had been a long time since Brody had been kissed by a girl. The week before his accident, Macy Anderson had kissed him at the bus stop after school. Seventeen years later, the woman Xander set him up with kissed him. Mainly so she could get close enough to steal his credit card. But compared to what just happened in his office, they hardly counted.

Brody didn't like to think about the parts of his life he had missed out on because of his father's temper. It wasn't only depressing, it was embarrassing. The burden of it grew with each passing year, making it harder to bear yet more critical to hide. So much so that not even his brothers knew the full extent of it.

But even as desperate as Brody was, getting what he wanted would require him to open himself up to someone. There was no way he could keep all of his secrets hidden. He would just have to decide what was more important if the moment ever arrived. So far, he hadn't had to choose.

Would Sam have kissed him if she knew he'd never...?

Brody shook his head. He wasn't going to taint the moment any more than it was already was. It was a milestone he wanted to savor, but he couldn't waste his time fantasizing about his secretary. Something more important had happened. It was bad timing that she'd come into his office at the worst possible moment. She'd seen *his* name on the computer screen.

He'd been so engrossed in his work that she could've driven a tractor through his office and he wouldn't have noticed. Between the time that he buzzed for the file and she brought it to him, his world had started to crumble. The day had come. The one he'd been anxiously waiting for. One of his web crawler queries had turned up something. Someone was looking for Tommy Wilder.

Damn it.

Just like the one that searched for Brody Butler, there was another crawler that sought out any interest in Tom, Thomas or Tommy Wilder. If someone, somewhere, was looking for him, Brody wanted to be the first to know. Once he assessed the risk, he and his brothers could determine what action needed to be taken. It was imperative that Tommy not be found and that questions not be asked about his current whereabouts.

That's because his location for the past sixteen years was a makeshift grave on the property where they grew up.

The Eden kids never talked about that day. It was as though they decided as a group that they could pretend it never happened if no one mentioned it ever again. They all went on with their lives, became successful and wealthy. But nothing they did or achieved could erase those memories. You can't forget the sight of that much blood. You just have to focus on other things.

That had worked for a long time. Then about a year ago, everything changed. Julianne had called in a panic last Thanksgiving when she discovered their parents had sold off a large portion of the family property. The part where Tommy was buried. All three plots were being developed and ran the risk of uncovering his remains.

The question was, which plot? Only his older brother Wade knew where Tommy's body was located and even then, after all this time, it was a good guess. They sprang into action and Wade returned to Cornwall to buy back the property. He'd been unsuccessful in his initial attempt, but given he was currently engaged to the woman that owned the land, the Eden children felt fairly secure that they'd retained control of the right plot and Tommy's body wouldn't be found.

All but Brody. And he hated to be proven right about these kinds of things.

Now that Sam had gone home for the day and he had finally quelled the distracting desire she stirred in him, he returned to the report on his machine. According to his records, someone had entered the search query *Tommy Wilder Cornwall Connecticut* with a variety of other keyword combinations including *jail, dead,* and *arrested.* Whoever was looking for Tommy didn't have a lot of faith in what he'd been doing the past sixteen years.

Fortunately, the person running the Google query was logged in under their Gmail account. In addition to the query details and results, it provided the IP address, internet provider, location and email address of the person running the search.

dwilder27. A Hartford, Connecticut, connection.

It would take a little legwork to figure out who this dwilder27 was and what he was after, but it was obvious he was a relative. Tommy had never been very forthcoming about his background. If he had family that might look for him, he kept that to himself. Brody wished he'd kept his hands to himself, too.

Fortunately, dwilder27's query hadn't pulled up any useful results. Mainly because Tommy couldn't get arrested in his current condition and no one knew he was dead. There was only an old, archived Cornwall news article about Tommy when he ran away from his foster home at the Garden of Eden Christmas Tree Farm. Molly and Ken had reported their oldest foster child as missing, but since his eighteenth birthday was the following week, not much effort went into the search. He was an adult and out of the system regardless of his location. End of story. For now.

Brody had queried Tommy periodically to make sure nothing else came up. As far as the internet was concerned, Tommy Wilder had vanished from the face of the earth. He hit the button to send the report to his home network and shut down his machines. He grabbed his coat, scooped up his laptop bag and headed for the elevator.

Passing through the multiple security measures he put in place was like a soothing ritual to him now, the barriers carefully crafted layers of protection. He was happy to be a ghost, an enigma. That was better than the reality.

A swipe of his badge and a scan of his thumbprint opened up the private elevator doors. On the ground floor, he turned away from the exit Sam and Agnes used to a narrow corridor. At the end was another door. A second badge swipe and rotating key code opened up his private entrance and exit to the building. Waiting for him was his car—a black Mercedes sedan with a tint job on the windows that was illegal in some states. He supposed he could've selected something flashier, but he didn't want to draw attention, just to block it out with the darkened glass.

As it was, he got a few looks from people who thought he might be *somebody*. They were wrong. He was nobody.

It was late to be heading home and traffic was easily navigated out of downtown Boston. Most people probably assumed that as an eccentric multimillionaire, he had some big loft apartment in the city, but nothing could be further from the truth. He'd opted for the exclusive and sprawling suburb of Belmont Hill. The lots were large and wooded, backing up to a bird sanctuary. Chris loved running around the backyard barking at the various birds that dared to light on the fence. Aside from that, it was a very quiet, secluded location. It made his home feel like a private retreat. It also helped that the neighbors kept to themselves.

It gave Brody the luxury of going outside from time to time during the day. He wasn't exactly an outdoorsy guy, but shooting hoops in his backyard and digging in his garden made him feel normal and boosted all that vitamin D synthesis. He could have wide-open windows letting light spill in and never worry about someone seeing him. That was something a home in the city could not provide.

The landscaping lights that highlighted the curve of his driveway were already on by the time he arrived. He enjoyed the fall, but the shorter days were hard because with his hours, he wouldn't see the sun at all.

Maybe that was part of what drew him to Sam. She was undoubtedly beautiful, but with her golden hair and bright smile, she was like her own source of sunshine. Simply having her at that desk would be enough to keep the winter blues away. She made him think of his roses.

Attached to the side of his home was a glass greenhouse. He had started growing roses in there a few years back. He didn't like watching his plants shrivel and die in winter. When it was cold and dreary, he needed their color and vibrancy as much as they needed the warmth. He had about twenty different varieties growing there, but his favorite was a dark pink hybrid tea rose called Miss All-American Beauty. Maybe he would take one to her tomorrow.

The click of toenails on the hardwood greeted him

as he came through the door. He wouldn't dare compare Sam to his golden retriever outside of his own mind, but he couldn't help smiling when he saw them both. Chris, of course, inspired Brody to throw a ball and scratch her belly. He had entirely different ideas where Sam was concerned.

On cue, Brody smiled as Chris skidded around the corner into the kitchen and then greeted her with an enthusiastic ear scratch. "How was your day?" he asked, anticipating no reply. "I had a great day and a terrible day all at once."

Chris sat down and cocked her head to one side while he spoke. Finally, she lifted a paw in the air and placed it sympathetically on his pant leg.

"More on that later, though. Let's get some dinner." He went through the routine of feeding the dog, reading his note from Peggy and plating up whatever dinner she'd left for him that night. Today was roasted lemon chicken and mashed potatoes with freshly shelled peas.

That handled, he headed into his office with his plate and his dog, ready to start research into the mysterious dwilder27.


"What is going on with you and this new job? You seem tense."

Sam looked up from her salad and found herself pinned by the knowing gaze of her best friend, Amanda. She'd avoided talking about her work at ESS. She didn't know what fell into the confidentiality agreement and what didn't, but it pained her to keep things from the friend she'd known since junior high. "What do you mean?"

"You've been really quiet lately. You haven't talked

about the new gig at all, which is weird considering how excited you were to finally get a break."

"I've just been busy," she said with a dismissive shake of her head. "My supervisor is very demanding."

"Who exactly are you working for at...?" Amanda paused with a frown. "Have you even told me where you're working?"

Sam didn't remember if she had. "Eden Software Systems." Certainly her working there wouldn't be a secret.

"How could you have not told me that yet?" Amanda's eyes lit up with unexpected excitement. She leaned over her lunch and spoke low. "Have you caught a glimpse of the mysterious CEO?"

This was definitely dangerous territory. "No. I don't have access to his floor," she lied.

"Oh, well," Amanda said with a sigh.

Her friend always kept up with celebrity gossip. Insider information on the most elusive CEO in history would be huge on the blogs. There was probably a bounty for details about Brody, but it wouldn't be enough to pay off the penalty of breaking her agreement.

"So what's got you all wound up?"

Sam bit at her lower lip. Now, more than ever, she needed girl talk. She wanted to confide in her best friend and figure out what to do. Maybe she could stay vague enough to talk but not tell too much. "I think I've done something stupid."

Amanda's fork paused in midair. "At work?" Sam nodded. "Well it can't be as bad as last time. You haven't slept with your new boss, have you?"

Her friend's blunt words might have stung if they

hadn't been so close to the truth. "I haven't slept with him. But I did kiss him yesterday."

Amanda rolled her eyes and shook her head. "This isn't a conversation for lunch. This is meant for Happy Hour with half-price wine." She eyed her iced tea with disdain. "What possessed you to kiss your boss? Did he come on to you?"

"No." And he hadn't. She had gone after him. Aggressively. Since almost the first day of work. "I kissed *him*. Frankly, he seemed a little stunned."

"Why on earth would you do that after that mess you went through before? This is the first job you've been able to land."

"I know. I'm not sure what I was thinking."

One of the perks of this job, however strange, should've been that her boss was a weird recluse who didn't come out of his office. Given she'd been fired for sleeping with her last manager, she should've been thrilled with the arrangement. The distance was a guaranteed buffer to ensure she couldn't make the same mistake twice. And yet she'd done everything she could to breach the barrier and coax the beast from its den. And then she'd kissed him.

Success felt bittersweet. First, she'd found a rose on her desk when she arrived this morning. A single pink rose stood on her desk in a tall silver bud vase. It was a deep fuchsia, her favorite shade of her favorite color, captured in her favorite flower. It was flawless, with silky petals that opened farther as the day went by. Brody didn't leave a note, but given no one else could get to this floor, there was no question from whom it had come. It was a romantic gesture. Not some over-the-top, massive bouquet. One single, perfect rose for one single, perfect kiss.

Then Brody had come out to see her twice this morning. He'd been surprisingly chatty, asking her about her evening and other pleasantries. Oddly enough, they'd both avoided the subjects of the kiss and the rose. Later, he had asked her—politely—to bring his lunch into his office before she went to meet Amanda, so she was able to enter his private space without being harassed.

Somehow, by invading his domain, she had tamed the beast. It was good and bad all at once.

"Is he married?"

"No," Sam said emphatically. She was pretty darn certain this time. He seemed too isolated for that, and Agnes had told her he was single. She would know. "And he's nothing like Luke. It's a completely different situation. But it complicates everything."

"Kissing your boss can do that. Here's a question for you, though—do you want to kiss him again?"

Sam took a deep breath and admitted the truth to herself. She did. It was so unproductive. So complicated. And yet she couldn't help the way he made her feel.

Her affair with her last boss had been purely physical. He was far too involved with himself to contribute any emotion to their relationship, and she was aware of it. It wasn't until later that she realized why. Brody was different. He aroused all the same physical desires, along with a protective instinct and emotional longings she couldn't ignore. Combined, it cranked up the intensity dial of her body to a point where she could barely concentrate when she was around him.

Brody was like an injured tiger. Dangerous, beautiful, fascinating…and yet, she couldn't fight the need to fix the hurt she saw in those blue eyes. Someone needed to be brave enough to go into his cage. Sam wanted to be the one. Even when she knew she could get bitten.

"I do," she finally said aloud.

"So, he's not married. He's not a sleaze. He's got a good job. You're interested in him, or you wouldn't want to kiss him a second time. If he's interested in you, what's the problem? This is a temporary job, after all."

Amanda always had a gift for cutting through the mental clutter to get to the heart of the issue. That's why Sam needed to talk to her so badly. She just wasn't sure it was that simple. Her body seemed to think so, but it had proven on more than one occasion that it couldn't be trusted. "I guess I'm worried it won't end well. I don't want to make the same mistake twice."

"Honey, I saw you go through that mess with Luke. I'm pretty sure you learned your lesson. Don't be so hard on yourself. If this guy really is different, you can't let that cloud your judgment. Take it slow. See what happens. You might be pleasantly surprised."

Sam eyed her watch and nodded. She needed to finish eating and head back to the office. "I will take all that under consideration."

Amanda smiled. "Keep me posted on the hot *seksi* times. I want every detail. I haven't dated anyone in months, and I need to live vicariously through *someone*."

They wrapped up lunch and Sam went back to work. The afternoon was busy, with Brody sending her multiple emails with tasks that kept her mind on work and off their situation. When she finally got the chance to glance at her clock, she realized it was time to go home for the day.

Yesterday after their kiss, she'd slunk away with her tail between her legs, too embarrassed to say goodbye. She wouldn't do that today, but she probably shouldn't initiate a lot of conversation as much as she wanted to.

She slung her magenta peacoat over her arm, scooped

up her brightly colored Dooney & Bourke purse and knocked gently at his door.

"Come in."

Sam turned the doorknob and stuck her head inside. Brody was seated at his main monitor, but he stood up when she entered so she could see more than his eyeballs over the top of it.

"Sam," he said with a smile she was getting rather used to seeing. "Do you have plans tonight?"

Her eyes widened, her jaw falling open. He was asking her out. It was Friday night. *Was* he asking her out? He talked to her, gave her a rose and now he was asking her out.

"Plans?" she repeated, not sure what her answer should be. "Not really. I was going to repaint my toenails and watch a sappy movie on the Hallmark channel. Why?" she added, unable to turn off the flirtatious response that was certain to get her in more trouble. "You got a better offer for me?"

Brody didn't respond right away. Any other man she knew would give her a sly grin and ask to take her out for a drink. He didn't seem to know how to react to her boldness. "Not really," he said with a frown. "I'm going to be working late tonight and I was wondering if you could stay for a while and help me with this briefing I'm presenting next week. I know it's Friday night and probably not your idea of a good time, but I could really use your help."

"Oh," Sam said, not sure if she was relieved or disappointed. "I thought you were asking me to dinner or something." She said the words without thinking, immediately regretting them the moment they left her mouth. Why would she even bring up the idea of them going on a date when he hadn't suggested it? Stupid.

Brody didn't notice her mental chastisement, as he seemed too busy trying to connect the pieces that would make her think such a thing. His eyes widened. "Oh, Sam, I'm sorry. I, uh…don't go out to dinner."

"Forget it," she said, wishing they both could.

"If you can stay tonight, I'll order Chinese for us. How about that?"

It wasn't the most romantic offer she'd ever received, but the overtime she'd be earning made up for it. "Sure." Sam tossed her things back onto her desk and returned to his office with the tablet he provided her to take notes.

About an hour later, the security desk called to let them know the Golden Dragon delivery guy was in the lobby. Sam didn't even know they had ordered yet. Brody hadn't asked her what she wanted. She could feel the heat of irritation at the back of her neck. She hated those arrogant men who ordered for a woman without thought to what she might actually want. "I'll be right back," she told him, leaving the office before she said something smart.

She returned a few minutes later with an increasingly poor attitude and a heavy sack of food. It was a good thing they weren't on a date. "What did you order?" she asked.

Brody had moved over to the living room sitting area so they could eat at the coffee table. He had already poured each of them a drink. "Kung Pao chicken, beef and broccoli, fried rice with no peas, hot and sour soup with extra wontons and vegetable eggrolls. Is that okay?"

Sam had been on the verge of telling him she didn't appreciate a guy choosing her food, but she had no complaints. He'd ordered everything just the way she would want it, down to no peas in the rice. Stunned into silence, she nodded, pulled a few cartons from the bag and set them on the glass table. They settled in and ate for a few minutes before she worked up the nerve to ask.

"How did you know what I wanted?"

"I looked it up," Brody said casually before crunching into an eggroll.

"Looked it up? My Chinese food preferences?"

Brody shrugged. "Everything can be found on the internet if you know where to look."

"Did you get it from that report you were running on me yesterday?" She'd been so flustered by his anger and the passionate kiss that followed that she forgot about seeing her own name on his computer. She wanted to know what that was all about. "Are you running a background check on me?"

Brody laughed. "Not yesterday. I ran a background check on you about a week before you even interviewed. Yesterday was merely a query to soothe my curiosity about you."

Sam stiffened slightly in her seat. How much did he know about her? Would her mistake with Luke show up in his file? It was a little unnerving to think about someone digging up every detail of her life from her credit score to her favorite foods. "You know, normal guys take a woman on a date and then ask her questions if they're curious. Running a background check is creepy."

"Creepy? Really?" He shrugged. "I see it as practical. Your way seems inefficient to me. The information I can find on my own is far more detailed and likely accurate than what I might get in person."

"Accurate? You think I'd lie to you about what kind of Chinese food I liked?"

"That's a bad example, but you could say you liked something you didn't just to be nice."

"But asking someone questions when you're on a date is more fun. And the street runs both directions," she added. "They get to know things about you, too." It would never occur to her to look on Google for information about Brody. Even if she didn't know there was nothing to find.

"As you can imagine, I don't date much. I'm far more comfortable with computers."

Sam set down her plate and leaned into Brody. "Do I make you uncomfortable?"

Brody swallowed hard, the thick cords in his neck moving up and down. He nodded. "A little. I'm not that good with people. Especially face to-face."

Sam was such a people person, she could hardly imagine living a secluded life like his. By the age of two, she was chatting up strangers in grocery stores and making friends with every kid on the playground. To her, computers were the complicated and unreasonable ones. "Well, the best way to improve is to practice. The more you're around me, the more comfortable you'll be."

His dark blue eyes focused on her for a moment, and then he shook his head. "You say that, but I don't find that to be entirely true. At least, with you."

Sam knew exactly what he meant. The more she was around Brody, the more restless and intrigued she became. He didn't think or react the way most men did. Everything he did was so calculated. Even when they kissed, she could tell he was stuck in his own head. He seemed to overthink everything, hesitating when he wasn't sure of the right course.

In a way, he reminded her of the boys in junior high

who couldn't decide if they wanted to kiss the girls or yank their ponytail. If a girl they liked actually spoke to them, they'd totally freeze up. Only this boy was thirty, in an expensive suit and had shoulders as broad as a Greek statue.

"That's normal," she admitted, "when you're getting to know someone new. Especially if you like them."

Brody diverted his eyes quickly back to his food, silently chewing and pondering her words. Sam did the same. She was nearly finished when he spoke again.

"I do like you, Sam. Would you be interested in having dinner with me tomorrow night, as well?"

Sam looked up from her plate of chicken and rice with surprise. More overtime? Well, she supposed she could put it into the bank in case it took a while to come across another job. Or she could get that new leather bag she'd drooled over in the window display at Saks Fifth Avenue. "Okay. What time do I need to be here?"

"Here?" Brody frowned and then nodded when he understood his mistake. "I'm not asking you to work over the weekend, Sam. I'm asking you to have dinner with me tomorrow night. A real date, like you suggested."

Had she suggested a date? "You said earlier that you don't go out to dinner." It was a stupid response, but it was the first thing that came to her mind.

Brody smiled. "I don't. That's why I'd like you to join me for dinner at my house."

# Five

"I should've said no. What was I thinking? I should've told him I had plans."

Sam sat muttering to herself in the back of the town car Brody sent to pick her up. The man behind the wheel paid no attention to her neurotic rambling. He'd hardly even spoken. He'd knocked on her door, introduced himself as her driver, Dave, and escorted her to the car. She told Brody she could drive herself, but he insisted it was difficult to find his house. To be honest, she'd never been in this area, so it was a good call. But that didn't mean she had to like it.

She couldn't change her mind and drive home, she thought with a sigh. If she chickened out in the driveway, it would be a long walk back. It was the right thing to do, wasn't it? As tempting as her handsome, brilliant, millionaire boss was, he was her *boss*. This couldn't end well.

And yet, Brody was nothing like Luke.

Sam had fought this battle with herself since she left the office Friday night. It might be the wrong choice, but the part of Sam that wanted to go on this date won. She wanted to see Brody outside of the office and all his barriers. To know what he was really like. She would be very disappointed to find retinal scanners in his home.

Sam had spent two hours getting ready. Half her closet was lying on the floor of her bedroom from going through her parade of options. She had finally decided on a champagne-colored pencil skirt with a black lace overlay, a black silk tank and lace shrug. She pulled her hair back into a clip to showcase her glittering gold chandelier earrings. Every inch of her body was scrubbed and painted and sparkled. She put on her most expensive perfume and her Sunday-go-to-meeting panties. These weren't the actions of a woman that didn't want to go on this date. She needed to silence the negative voice in her head and enjoy her night.

The car slowed and turned onto a narrow neighborhood street. Sam looked out the window at the houses they passed. They were huge. Each one was more of an estate than a home, on a plot of land big enough to fit nearly fifty of her apartments on their lawns. They'd passed about ten homes before they turned into a long, circular driveway. "We're here, ma'am."

This was it. The moment she'd looked forward to and dreaded all day. Her heart started racing in her chest, but she had to get out of the car when the driver opened the door. She took a deep breath, grabbed her clutch and stepped out onto the cobblestone drive. "Thank you," she said.

The driver nodded and pulled away before she could turn back. She faced the sprawling home, admiring the

lighting that made the shrubs and trees glow golden. It
was multileveled and L-shaped with a three-car garage
at the end of the driveway. A covered patio ran along
the front, sheltering a few rocking chairs. It wasn't at
all like she expected except for the tiny surveillance
cameras pointing to the front door and to where she
was standing. That was more like the Brody she knew.

She hadn't taken a single step when the front door
opened and a big yellow dog charged straight for her.
The animal was at least eighty pounds, and Sam had
nothing but a beaded purse to defend herself. Running
was impossible in the four-inch Stuart Weitzman heels
she'd chosen for tonight. She could only close her eyes
and brace herself for the mauling.

Instead there was the thump of heavy paws against
the lapel of her wool coat and a wet glide along her
cheek. The weight sent her stumbling back on her heels.
She misstepped on the uneven cobblestones and before
she could right herself, she and the dog toppled back
into a mulch flower bed.

"Chris!"

Sam opened her eyes to find herself nose-to-nose
with a golden retriever. She struggled to push aside the
overly affectionate canine and get up, but she was no
match for its enthusiasm.

"Chris*tina!*" A man's voice shouted again, this time
closer and more sternly.

The dog was jerked away a second later, and Sam
looked up to see an apologetic Brody hovering over
her. He held out his hand to help her up. "I am so sorry.
Chris is harmless. She was more excited to see a new
person than I expected."

Sam stood up, dusting the wood chips from her lace

pencil skirt and subtly rubbing her bruised rear. "Chris is apparently not as antisocial as you are."

"Not at all. Are you okay? Did you twist your ankle or anything?"

"No, no," she said dismissively. "The only thing hurt is my pride."

Brody smiled and Sam couldn't help but do the same. It was amazing how quickly she had been able to see past the scars. That charming smile and those soulful blue eyes made the rest just fade into the background.

And then he turned to look down the street. A car was coming toward the house. Sam watched with disappointment as his smile faded in the shine of the oncoming headlights. He was so worried about people seeing him. Sam had seen him. He was growing more comfortable with her by the second, but it appeared that she was a notable exception. Brody was far from strolling through a shopping mall filled with people, or even meeting face-to-face with his own employees.

"Let's get inside," he said, reaching his hand out to her.

She accepted it, a tiny thrill running through her as she walked beside Brody up the stairs to the front door. Sam was stunned the moment she walked in. The outside of his home wasn't nearly as surprising as the inside. It wasn't what she expected at all. The house was bright and open with light oak floors and white trim. The walls were a soft mocha color. The living room furniture was cream with plush rugs and large windows that ran nearly floor to ceiling.

Brody stopped and turned around when her hesitation pulled her hand from his. "Is something wrong?"

Sam immediately felt guilty for thinking he lived in some kind of dark cave. "No, I just…it wasn't what

I was expecting. It's very different from your office, I mean."

He nodded, helped her out of her coat and hung it on a brass hook inside the entryway. "Come with me to the kitchen. Dinner is about ready," he said. "I feel a little more comfortable out here than I do in town. There's no one that can see in."

"No one can get into your office, either. You could paint it purple with pink polka dots and no one would see it. I mean, who even cleans it?"

"I do. I don't trust anyone else to go in there and for good reason. The security measures and tinted windows are there because more than a few journalists have tried to hitch their careers to exposing me. My security team caught one posing as a window washer not long ago. Another tried to apply to housekeeping thinking they could get to me. Keeping my office dark and locked up is the only thing that keeps me from being exposed."

"What about here?"

"No one knows about this place. My home is owned by a shadow holding company with no public tie to me or ESS. I, of course, own the company, but no one knows that. And no one but my immediate family and a few people on my payroll has ever stepped foot on the property, so there's no chance of a leak."

Sam swallowed hard. Somehow she'd managed to not only make it into the beast's secret lair, she'd gotten into his private retreat. And this time by invitation. She didn't know if she should be flattered or terrified. "I'm honored, I think, that you trust me enough to invite me over. I'd never reveal that information, of course."

"You've got five million good reasons not to." He smiled.

Sam shrugged. "I wouldn't tell anyway."

"I know. I wouldn't have asked you on a date and brought you here if I thought otherwise. Come on, dinner should be done any second now."

Sam followed Brody down the hallway, noticing as he walked ahead of her that he was wearing nicely snug jeans and a blue plaid button-down shirt that was left untucked. He was also barefoot. It was the first time she'd seen him in something other than a power suit and she liked it. It was a very sexy look for him. He appeared relaxed and comfortable in a way he never seemed to be at the office.

She rounded a corner and walked into a large, spacious kitchen with cream-colored cabinets and butcher block countertops. It was a chef's dream, or so she imagined. Sam wasn't much of a cook, but she got by. A place this luxurious would be wasted on her limited culinary abilities.

Dinner was in progress with several pots on the six-burner gas stove and bowls scattered around the counters. For some reason, she hadn't expected him to actually cook, even though he'd invited her over for dinner. Given his affection for takeout, she didn't picture him as the kind of man who was very comfortable in the kitchen.

Brody poured a glass of white wine for each of them and held one out for her. She accepted it gratefully. "You're cooking," she said with surprise lacing her words. Sam sniffed delicately at the air. "What are we having? It smells like cheese and…charcoal."

Brody's eyes widened for a moment. He quickly spun on his heel, turned to the set of double ovens mounted in the wall and frowned. A cloud of black smoke rolled out of the top oven as he quickly snatched out a charred cookie sheet with a dark crusty bundle in the center.

He dropped the contents into the trash and tossed the pan into the sink to cool. "Well, it was supposed to be a chicken roulade with goat cheese, sundried tomatoes and spinach."

Sam switched on an overhead fan to disperse the smoke so the smoke detectors didn't go off. "Sounds good."

"Yeah," he said with dismay as he examined the controls and the recipe on the counter beside it. "If I had put the oven on three-fifty instead of four-fifty, it would've been."

Sam drowned her giggles in a sip of wine. "A computer genius that can't set the temperature on a digital stove?"

"Give me some credit," he said with a laugh. "As a kid, I was the only one in the house that could program the VCR." Brody rested his hands on his hips and looked around the kitchen with a frustrated pinch to his brow. Sam could see the CEO in him wanting to start firing off orders to deal with the situation. Unfortunately, tonight he was a corporation of one.

"My housekeeper offered to make us dinner tonight," he admitted, running his fingers through his hair. "I told her no, I wanted to cook for you myself. I guess she didn't have as much faith in my culinary skills as I did, and rightly so."

"Do you cook much?"

Brody shook his head. "Almost never. Peggy leaves dinner for me every night. But I wanted to impress you, and I figured following a recipe would be easy enough. I can't take you to an expensive restaurant, so it seemed like a nice touch. Now we're going to have to order pizza. I don't have enough stuff left over to make it again."

Sam smiled and made her way over to the Sub-Zero refrigerator. They wouldn't be eating pizza if she had anything to say about it. "Don't give up on us quite yet."

Brody was amazed. He knew from working with Sam that she was smart, efficient and innovative. But seeing her at work in his own kitchen was an entirely different matter. She had taken charge of the situation, and he had to admit that it was a huge turn-on. He could only sit back and watch as she kicked off her heels, slipped out of her lace shrug and took his kitchen by storm.

Chris sat down beside him to watch her work, as well. She ran the risk of getting stepped on if she got into Sam's way. Brody patted her head and sipped his wine, answering questions as he was asked where one thing or another was. He enjoyed watching her work. It was much better in person than watching her from his surveillance monitors. She was full of color, moving with a gracefulness and ease. Occasionally she would look over at him with a smile that was so brilliant it would make it hard to breathe.

It was difficult for him to tear his eyes away from the seam of her stockings that lined the back of her shapely legs and disappeared under her fitted lace skirt. He wanted to interrupt her work to press her against the cold steel of the refrigerator. He wanted to know what it would feel like to let his hands glide over those silk stockings. He wasn't that hungry, anyway.

Before he could make a move, Sam turned triumphantly toward him with a second, unburned dinner made. She carried two plates to the oval table in the breakfast nook where he was sitting. There were marinated chicken breasts she'd cooked on the grill set into his range and angel hair pasta tossed with olive oil, garlic, herbs and parmesan cheese. With them, she'd paired the green salad and garlic bread he hadn't ruined from their first menu.

"It looks wonderful," he said, admiring her hard work and the flush of her cheeks from activity. "I feel bad, though. I invited you to dinner and you ended up cooking."

Sam smiled and shook her head. "It was fun."

"You really seemed to be in your element. Do you like to cook?"

At that, Sam laughed. "Actually, no. And to be honest, I'm not really a very good cook, either, so don't put away the takeout menu yet. But I know enough not to go hungry. It was a necessity when I was younger. My dad became a single father overnight. He was so unprepared for everything that came with it, especially handling mischievous twin boys and the girliest little girl on the planet. He had his hands full and I knew it, so I tried to help out where I could. My dad was a horrible cook. My brothers and I would've starved if I hadn't stepped up and shoved Dad away from the stove."

Brody recalled the background investigation he'd done on Sam. It said her mother had died when she was seven. He remembered that now. But he knew better than to mention it. Instead, he cut into his chicken and took a bite. "This is great. My mother wasn't a very good cook. She tried, but it never came out quite right. When she overcooked things my father would get so angry at her."

And him. And the dog. And anyone else who got in his way when he was in a rage.

"My mom was a great cook. At least that's what I remember. I was seven when she died. She had been letting me help around the kitchen with little tasks at dinnertime, but I certainly wasn't prepared to take over. It didn't stop me, of course. Things had to get done. It might not be the best tasting food or the smoothest ironing job, but I tried. That's why my dad always called me 'Daddy's Little Fixer.' From a very young age, I've had this drive to fix everything."

"Sounds like a harmless compulsion."

Sam swallowed her own bite of food and chased it with some wine. He could tell she was trying to cover a frown. He watched as a blond curl came loose from her hair clip and tumbled down along her cheek. Brody wanted to reach out and gently wrap the golden silk around his finger. He imagined it would feel as soft as her lips had.

Sam absentmindedly tugged the loose strand behind her ear and continued talking. "You'd think so, but not always. My brothers weren't always as appreciative of my help. They prefer to call me the Meddler. Apparently, I don't know when to stop or mind my own business. I just get this idea in my head of how things should be and I can't ignore the problem. I have to fix it."

Brody watched the woman he'd allowed to breach his inner sanctum as she continued to eat. This dating thing was going okay so far. He was learning about her and sharing some of himself, like she'd described. They'd worked together to overcome a minor crisis. The boxes on his date checklist were being checked off, one by one. If he managed not to do something stupid to run her off, this might be a really great night. He enjoyed Sam's company, which was something he couldn't say for most people. She was everything he'd always hoped for in a woman. Sam was smart and funny, beautiful and caring. She hadn't seemed very interested in his money, either.

From the monitor in his office he'd watched her eyes light up with delight at receiving that single rose just as if she'd received a hundred roses. Or diamonds. And most importantly, she looked him in the eye with the flame of desire instead of disgust.

What he couldn't put his finger on was what she saw in him if money wasn't the draw. It was one thing to be polite and friendly at work to develop a good rapport. But why had she kissed him? Or agreed to this date? She didn't have to do any of that. Or perhaps she did. Maybe this was it. Was he only a project to her? "Are you going to fix me?" he asked.

She looked at him then, her wide dark eyes searching his face for something. He expected her to blow off the question, lie about it outright or make a joke. He knew that most people in his life disapproved of his lifestyle. If Molly, his foster mother, could tell him what to do again, things would be very different, he was sure. For someone with an itch to help like Sam, he was surprised she hadn't broken into hives restraining herself.

But she didn't dismiss the question. Instead she looked him straight in the eye and said, "Fix what?"

At that, he almost laughed. "Fix what?" he asked, getting up from the table to put his empty plate in the sink. "Come on, now. I'm a grouchy, scarred hermit. You're the first woman to step into this house that isn't related or paid to clean it. Certainly you've come across something about me that you're dying to put right."

Sam followed him through the kitchen and smiled reassuringly when he turned back to her. "All that stuff is on the outside. I'm not worried about that apart from how it impacts you on the inside." Her hand rested gently on his chest, over his heart.

Brody's blood started pumping furiously through his veins at her touch. His heart beat so hard, he was certain she could feel it pounding against her fingertips. Her innocent gesture had lit a fire inside him. The heat of it spread through his body like warm honey and caused every muscle to tense with anticipation.

"You're a brilliant businessman. A computer genius. A strong leader for your company. You have amassed more money and power in a few short years than most people will in a lifetime. You do the work you love. I'm sure your life isn't perfect, but whose is? Everyone has their own tolerance and thresholds of what they can live with. From where I sit, I don't know what I could do to make your life better."

"You could kiss me." Brody said the words before he could lose his courage. She saw him as decisive and bold. He needed to be tonight if he was going to get what he wanted. And whether or not he should, he wanted her. More than he'd wanted any other woman in his life.

He took her hand in his, pulling it away from his chest and wrapping his other arm around her waist. He tugged her against him, sprawling his palm across her lower back.

Sam looked up at him in surprise, and then a coy smile curled her lips. She pressed into him, bringing her hand behind his neck to tease at his collar. "I think I can do that," she said, climbing up onto her toes.

Brody dipped his head down and closed the gap between their heights. Without her heels on, she was more petite than he anticipated. Their lips met in a soft, tender kiss. He relished the feel of her fingertips against the stubble of his jaw and the gentle, probing glide of her tongue along his own. It was an easy movement, one he didn't have to think too much about. But Brody was a strategist, and he was always focusing on his next move instead of enjoying the moment like he should.

He was lost in his own thoughts when Sam thrust her tongue into his mouth. She crushed her breasts against the wall of his chest, cranking up the intensity between them. The movement sent a jolt of electricity down his spine, urging him on. On instinct, he backed her against the kitchen island, pressing his body into hers. His hands planted on the countertop, flanking her waist. It was easier than trying to figure out which part of her he wanted to touch next.

Their kiss was no longer sweet, nor gentle. Sam's hands roamed across his chest, her fingernails scratching the coarse fabric of his shirt and teasing the muscles beneath it. Her touch coaxed an ache of desire that strained against his tight jeans. He pressed himself against her stomach and swallowed a deep groan of pleasure. It came out like a growl vibrating in his throat.

The feeling echoed through Brody's entire body. She felt so amazing against him. His mind started racing again. Was this *it*? Could this really be happening after all this time? He thought he was reading the signals correctly. With every nerve in his body, he prayed for it to be true.

"I want you so badly," he whispered against her lips. "Say yes. Stay with me tonight."

Brody could feel a stiffness settle into Sam's muscles, and then she pulled away from his kiss. The few inches between them brought a rush of cool air that helped him regain some control. She looked at him, her brow gently furrowing into a V. There was a hesitation, a worry there, and he didn't know how to make it go away. He couldn't lose her after getting this close. He wouldn't let her go. If she walked out the door, his chance with her might have passed forever. He wanted Sam more than he'd ever wanted a woman before. No matter what it took, what he had to expose of himself, he would do what he had to do to keep her here with him.

"Please, Samantha."

When she looked away, she shook her head just enough to send his heart sinking into his gut. The hands that had caressed him a moment before were now pushing gently at his chest. He took a step back. Somehow, he'd ruined it.

"I'm sorry, Brody. I can't."

# Six

Sam watched the conflicting emotions fly across Brody's face. He tried hard to hide them, but she could see his disappointment. Could he see hers? Would he be able to understand how much she wanted him but feared having him at the same time?

"I should probably go. Dave gave me his card so I could call when I was ready to leave."

"Don't leave, not yet." His voice was low but even. He wasn't demanding or even begging. "Peggy made a cobbler for us, and I have French vanilla ice cream. We can eat it out on the patio."

"I don't know, Brody." Dessert, although it sounded nice, would only be putting off the inevitable. She was either going to go home or sleep with Brody. So she probably should just go ahead and go.

"It's cherry," he added, his blue eyes a little hopeful as he watched her reaction. "I won't touch you again unless you ask me to. I promise."

Sam sighed. Her resistance was wearing down, fast. "It's not that I don't want you to touch me, Brody."

"Then you don't want cobbler?"

"No, I would love some cobbler. I just—"

"Great." Brody turned away, cutting off her excuses and pulling a carton of ice cream from the freezer. On the counter was a deep casserole dish covered in foil. He lifted the top to reveal a golden flaky crust with deep red cherry juices oozing along the edges.

She wanted to grab his arm and insist that she really had to leave. *Right now.* But Sam really loved cherries. And if she was honest with herself, she didn't want to go home. She was having a good time. She was only worried things were moving too quickly.

Brody dished them both out a bowl with a scoop of ice cream on top. The cobbler was still warm enough to start the vanilla immediately melting into a pool over the top. "Here," he said, handing her the dish. "We can talk about whatever it is outside."

It was then that she realized how chilly it had gotten lately. Boston had stayed unseasonably warm for the area until the day before yesterday. With the sun having set an hour or so ago, the night air would have a definite chill. Not exactly the right weather for eating ice cream on the porch. "Isn't it too cold out? It's October."

He shook his head. "I've got it under control."

Sam followed him through the maze of the house, admiring the winding central staircase and the museum-quality artwork on the walls that wrapped around it. They passed an area that looked like his office and then a den with a large television and comfortable chairs. There were French doors leading off to a covered patio.

When she stepped out onto the deck, she was greeted with an unexpected blast of warm air. Perched on each side of the seating area were tall gas torch heaters, and a third flame roared from a massive stone fireplace. It continued on into an outdoor kitchen that wrapped around the deck and down into the yard.

Beyond them was a swimming pool. It shimmered a deep turquoise-blue in the darkness, the steam from the heated water rising up in the cool night. There were massive trees and bushes flanking the yard, some adorned with tiny fairy lights. To the left was a glass enclosure that glowed with a golden light. The heat inside had fogged up the windows, but she could see the dark green foliage and pops of bright colors inside. A greenhouse. Perhaps where he'd grown her rose?

It was all so beautiful. The perfect yard for throwing parties, oddly enough, although it could also be considered the perfect private retreat from the world.

Brody was standing beside the fireplace holding their dessert. "Do you like it? Is it warm enough?"

"It's beautiful. And quite toasty, thank you."

Sam sat down in the outdoor love seat directly across from the fireplace and accepted her dessert. Brody sat beside her. She expected him to start pressing her for answers regarding her abrupt about-face, but he appeared content to eat his cobbler and enjoy her company. Even Chris curled up in front of the fireplace with a rawhide bone and started happily munching on it.

It wasn't until her spoon scraped the bottom of the empty bowl that Brody spoke again. "So, talk to me, Sam. Did I do something?"

"What makes you think you did something wrong?"

Brody settled his bowl on the table and turned so he was facing toward her as he spoke. "This is uncharted territory for me here. I'm not so arrogant as to think I might not misstep."

"You mean you've never seduced one of your employees?" It was a fairly direct and prying question, but she needed to know if this was something he did often. If she'd asked Luke that question, it might've saved her a lot of heartache and time at the unemployment office. If he'd answered honestly.

It was a serious question, but Brody started laughing. And continued to laugh. It went on for so long that Sam began to get irritated.

"Hey!" she said, snapping his attention back to her. "I'm serious."

"I know, and I'm sorry. But you do realize the only two employees I've seen in person since I started this company are Charlie, the head of security, and Agnes, right?"

At that, even Sam had to smother a giggle. Charlie was sixty with a bristly, mostly gray beard and a rapidly expanding beer belly. Civilian life had been a rough adjustment for the former Army intelligence officer. And then, of course, her godmother, Agnes. She was in her fifties, married since near birth and looked more like a stern Sunday school teacher than a romantic outlet for Brody.

"Fair enough," she admitted. It did make her feel better to know he didn't make a habit of this, even if only for a lack of opportunity. But it didn't change things between the two of them.

"Have you ever slept with your supervisor?"

Brody turned the question around on her, and the time for laughing was over. "Yes," Sam said, struggling to swallow the knot in her throat. "And it ruined my career and damn near my whole life."

Brody sighed and leaned back against the cushions of the love seat. She could tell he hadn't expected that serious of an answer from her. At least *that* hadn't shown up in her background check. Everyone at her office knew the truth, but the HR records were squeaky-clean, probably to protect Luke. "Tell me what happened," he said.

Sam didn't want to rehash all of this tonight, but she could see the determination etched into Brody's face. He had a solid dose of "fix-it" in him, too. "I was new to the company, and I was hired as the administrative support to the head of marketing. His name was Luke. I was immediately taken under his spell. He was movie-star handsome. He dressed well and smelled amazing. He was so nice to me, too. When he asked me to accompany him on a business trip, I was thrilled. I didn't expect something to happen between us, but when it did, I was powerless to fight it. Away from the office, he was such a romantic. We spent each day working and each night making love in his suite."

She felt stupid admitting to this out loud. "I would've believed almost anything that man said. And that was a mistake. He was married. To the woman that headed up the finance department, of all people."

"You never suspected he was married?"

Sam shook her head. "I know it sounds ridiculous. But I swear to you he never mentioned her. He didn't have a single photograph of his family in his office or a wedding ring on his hand. I had no reason to think he might be..." Her voice drifted off.

"Anyway, one day we were in his office and he had me pressed against the filing cabinet. We were just messing around—I would never have slept with him at work—but his wife came in and caught us. She blew a gasket. The next thing I knew, people were whispering as I went into the break room and I had become the woman that climbed the career ladder on her knees. I was laid off a few weeks later. Wouldn't you know that the finance department determined that marketing was suddenly overstaffed?"

Brody's jaw tightened as he listened to her tell her story. He seemed angry. Sam hoped it wasn't at her for being so stupid and naive. "Didn't anyone realize what was really going on?"

"If they did, they didn't care. I was a home wrecker, out on my rear end, and couldn't get a reference to save my soul. This job working for you is the first thing I've been able to land. And I only managed that because of Agnes, I'm sure."

Brody leaned into her but didn't reach for her. "What happened to you was terrible. That Luke guy should be strung up by his junk. But let me ask you something… do you really think I'm going to sleep with you and toss you out onto the street like he did?"

Sam felt a flush of embarrassment rise to her cheeks. "No…and yes. It's a hard-learned lesson, Brody. I'm already a temporary employee. Easy to get rid of. And if you sleep with one boss, it's a fluke. Twice…and it's a bad habit. I don't want to make the same mistakes."

Brody's hand came to rest heavily on her shoulder. His touch was warm and the massaging motion of his fingertips made her want to close her eyes and curl up in his lap.

"Sam, let me assure you first that I am not married. Not even close. No serious girlfriends or fiancées tucked away, either. I am very, *very* single. Two, I am not a sleaze. Please don't think for a moment that I'm trying to use my position as your supervisor to pressure you into something you don't want to do. I don't ever want to make you uncomfortable. Here, or at work."

"Thank you." Sam knew what he was saying was

true. She'd been telling herself that since the first buzz of attraction between them. She was just scared to get burned again.

"And finally...I want you to understand that I'm not the kind of guy that casually sleeps around with women. I really like you, Sam. You're beautiful and smart and funny." Brody reached out to caress her cheek. "You look at me—really look at me—when no one else does. I don't think you truly understand how rare that is in my life. I don't need coded doors and thumbprint scanners to keep people away. They stay away on their own.

"Since my accident, no one looks at me the way they did before. It was so hard, living my life every day and dealing with the stares and the reactions of people. I was just a kid, Sam. When I got old enough, I started my company and hid away because I didn't want to deal with it anymore. It's my choice to keep people away now. But in shutting away the bad, I shut away the good, too. It was probably a mistake. It has cost me so much of my personal life, but I did what I thought I had to do to protect myself."

Sam's heart ached listening to his story, but she didn't quite grasp where he was headed with the conversation.

"It might be unheard of in this day and age, Sam, but...I'm still a virgin."

Brody had never spoken those words aloud to another living soul. Not even his brothers knew the truth. They thought he'd lost it to a working girl they'd all chipped in and bought him after high school. And he let them believe it. It was easier than telling them that even their well-paid whore couldn't look him in the eye when she touched him.

He'd walked away from her without regrets. Getting laid would be nice, but he wanted more. Call him a hopeless romantic, but it was true. He wanted companionship. Intimacy. Love. Until now, Brody hadn't met a woman who might be interested in him for anything but his money. He hadn't come across anyone who inspired him to open up and expose his demons to her.

Sam had come so close. He didn't want her to walk away and he'd decided that telling her the truth might be the only thing to convince her he wasn't like other men. But it may have backfired. He was pretty sure by the extended silence between them that he'd driven her away with his blunt confession instead.

Brody held his breath. Sam's mouth had dropped open slightly when he'd spoken, but she hadn't moved since then. She was watching him. Probably thinking about how to gracefully get out of this uncomfortable situation. He was on the verge of giving her an out when she set her cobbler bowl on the table and stood up. His stomach sank. She was leaving.

Him and his big mouth.

But she didn't go. Instead, she reached out to him. He took her hand and she tugged until he stood up. He looked down at her with his brow drawn in confusion as she stepped close to him and wrapped her arms around his waist. She rested her head against his chest and sighed.

The feel of her pressed against him was amazing. He swallowed a groan as every inch of her soft body molded against his own. He hesitated to touch her. If this was just a pity hug and she would be out the door in a moment, he didn't want to let himself fall into it. And if he did, he was afraid that it might send her running again. But he simply couldn't help touching her. He enveloped her in his arms and pressed his lips against the golden curls at the crown of her head.

He didn't want to let her go, yet before he was ready, he could feel Sam pull back.

A sly smile curled her lips as she looked up at him, her body still pressed against his. "I can fix that," she said at last.

For a moment, Brody couldn't quite piece together what she meant by that. Of course, it was hard to think with her breasts pressing against his chest. She couldn't possibly mean…? His mind backed up. He'd said he was a virgin, and she said she could fix that. He swallowed hard and took Sam's face into his hands. "Are you sure?" he asked. "I mean, are you doing this because you want to, or because you have this need to fix—"

Sam didn't respond to his question. Instead, she climbed to her toes, pressed her mouth against his and silenced him. Her lips were soft and warm, and this time, she tasted like cherry cobbler instead of cherry lip gloss. He lost himself in the kiss, his thumbs stroking the smooth skin of her jaw.

When Sam pulled away, she took Brody's hand in hers and started walking back into the house. He followed her inside, and when she paused at the staircase, he nodded. At the top of the winding stairs, he pushed ahead of her and led the way to his master suite.

As he opened the double French doors that led to his bedroom, his heart started pounding so loudly in his ears he was certain Sam could hear it. He kept turning a nervous gaze her way, but she just smiled and followed him without concern.

He paused in the center of the space. His king-size bed was on the right, facing a wall of windows that gave him the perfect view of the sunrise every morning. Past it was a small sitting area with a fireplace and the entrance to the master bathroom.

"So, this is my room," he began as he turned to face Sam, not quite sure of the best approach to take from here. He hated feeling so awkward at this when he was able to confidently take charge in so many other areas of his life.

Sam had no question of how to proceed. Her dark eyes looked into his own as her fingers went to his collar. On reflex, his hand shot to cover hers and halt the movement.

Sam gasped softly at his sudden movement. "What's the matter?" she asked, her dark eyes wide with concern.

Brody closed his eyes and swallowed hard. What would he tell her? That he wanted to leave his shirt on during sex? That he wanted the lights out? It sounded ridiculous in his mind, much less said aloud. Was it worse than admitting the truth? That as badly as he wanted her, he didn't want her or anyone else to see what his bastard of a father had done to him?

Some people might have seen Brody's face, but no one outside of a hospital had ever seen his chest. Even as a kid sharing a room with Wade, he always kept covered. He came out of the bathroom fully dressed after a shower. He never went swimming with the other boys. They probably expected him to have more scars from his accident, but Brody didn't want anyone to know the full extent of what his father had inflicted on him long before that last day.

"Nothing. I just…" His voice trailed off. Brody wanted Sam more than he wanted to hide, but his sense of self-preservation was deeply ingrained in his every response. "I want you so badly. But I don't want you to see—"

"I don't want you hiding from me, Brody. There's nothing that you could show me to make me want you any less."

She seemed to know. Even with his shirt still buttoned, Sam knew what he was hiding. Brody let go of her hand and let her continue. She watched his expression with unmatched intensity as inch by inch of chest was exposed. He tensed, holding his breath as his shirt opened and she pushed it over his shoulders. He watched and waited for the reaction he dreaded. She might think she meant what she said, but she hadn't seen all his scars yet.

Sam paused only a moment in taking in the hard lines of his chest to follow the trail of rippled skin that ran down his shoulder and over the heart that beat like a bass drum in his rib cage. Then her palm went to it. Sam covered his heart with her hand and then traveled the path back up his neck to touch the scarred side of his face.

Brody fought the urge to pull away from her touch. He always pulled away. He didn't like the idea of anyone touching his scars. His injuries were bad enough to look at, even more distressing to feel. Sam didn't seem to agree. She was determined to challenge his every barrier. There wasn't the slightest flinch of disgust as she cupped his cheek and drew his mouth to hers.

He kissed her again, the thoughts of his scars fading away. It was done. She hadn't run. Now he could try to focus on other things. His hands moved to her waist, gliding easily over the slick fabric of her top. His fingers pulled at the material, tugging it out from the waist of her skirt so he could make contact with her bare skin. Unlike Brody with his rough scars, Sam's skin was flawless and silky soft to the touch. She was delicate and feminine and beautiful, so different from himself. He loved the feel of her against his palms as they ran over her back and around her sides to brush the edge of her rib cage.

Sam gasped against his lips and pulled away. Brody froze in his tracks and frowned nervously. "What did I do?"

She shook her head and smiled. "Nothing. Your hands are just a little cold for such a sensitive spot."

"I'm sorry."

"I can take care of it," she said. In one fluid movement, her arms twisted around her torso and pulled her top up and over her head.

Brody's mouth went dry as a desert when he was faced with the sight of her breasts confined in a black lace bra. They were large and full, threatening to spill over the scalloped edge of the cups that were stitched with tiny crystals. She was a buxom pin-up girl come to life in his bedroom. He tried to swallow, but the lump in his throat stayed stubbornly in place.

Sam reached behind herself and unfastened her bra. It dropped to the floor, exposing the very things he'd been admiring. They were lovely. Brody had seen his share of breasts in magazines and movies, but they didn't prepare him for this moment. The full pale globes had tight pink tips. He ached to touch them but couldn't make himself move.

Sam reached out and took both of his wrists in her hands. She brought them up to her mouth and blew hot air across his palms. The feel of her breath on his skin sent a sizzle up his arms, but when she brought the heated palms down to cover each breast, the sizzle turned into a jolt.

He watched as Sam closed her eyes and indulged in the feel of his hands on her. His palms grazed over the tips, his fingertips pressing into her flesh. Sam made a soft hum of pleasure in her throat as he teased and explored her skin. But he wanted to taste them, too. His head dipped to take a nipple into his mouth.

Sam gasped and arched her back, pressing her breasts even harder against his touch. Her skin was both sweet and salty against his tongue. He drank her in, drawing hard at one breast and then the other, lightly flicking his tongue over the swollen pink tips. She squirmed in his arms, lacing her fingers in the curls at the nape of his neck and tugging him closer. Her reaction urged him on, building confidence in him as he tried different ways to make her cry out with pleasure.

Brody only pulled away when he felt the graze of her touch at the fly of his jeans. With sure fingers, Sam unbuttoned and unzipped, slowly backing him toward the bed. When his calves met with the emerald-green brocade comforter, her hand slipped beneath the elastic of his waistband. Her fingers curled around his firm heat, sending a shockwave of sensation through his body.

"Oh, damn," he groaned and reached back to the bed to steady himself.

She pressed against his chest with her other hand, easing him to sit against the edge of the mattress. He braced himself with both arms propped behind him. Sam tugged at the jeans, pulling them and his briefs down his legs. Lying naked with Sam crouched down between his legs was a surreal experience. He'd never felt so exposed in his life. And yet with Sam it was different. It wasn't like going out in public and having people stare. It was exhilarating.

With the last of his clothes tossed to the side, Sam knelt down and reached for him again. She stroked him slowly, running her thumb from the base to the tip. Brody wanted to watch, but he couldn't keep his eyes from closing and savoring the feeling. He wanted to remember every sensation of this night.

Sam caught him by surprise when she took him into her mouth. His lids flew open, a shudder running through his whole body as the hot, wet heat of her mouth moved over him. It took every ounce of control he had to keep from going over the edge when she touched him like that. But damn, it felt amazing.

It was no wonder people seemed to be so obsessed with sex everywhere he turned. Brody had been seriously missing out all these years.

Finally, he had to put a stop to it or this would be over before it truly began. "Sam," he managed in a hoarse whisper. "Stop. I can't…" he said, curling tight wads of the comforter in his fists. "Please."

When she pulled away, he was both relieved and disappointed, but neither feeling lasted for long. He watched her stand up and unzip her skirt. It shimmied over her hips and fell to the floor. Beneath it she wore a pair of matching black lace panties and thigh-high stockings. She put one foot on the edge of the bed, watching his face as she rolled the stocking down her leg. When she switched to take off the other stocking, he caught a flash of pink flesh peeking out from beneath her flimsy panties.

Sam knew it, too. He got the feeling she was doing it on purpose. She smiled as she threw the other stocking aside. She took a step away, allowing him the full view of her body, then turned around. The luscious round curves of her backside were accented by the high cut of her thong panties and the tiny crystal heart stitched at the top. She glanced seductively over her shoulder at him, hooked her thumbs beneath the lace and drew her panties down over her hips. Brody couldn't tear his eyes away as the fabric inched lower, sliding down her shapely legs.

Lastly, she reached up behind her head and unclipped her hair clasp. The mess of blond curls rained down over her shoulders and back as she shook her head. Then she turned around and faced him.

She was the most beautiful thing he'd ever seen in his life. Powerfully seductive, curvaceous, feminine... And she was crawling, naked, over him until she was straddling his waist and looking down at him. His hands went to her hips, stroking the soft skin and steadying their nervous shaking.

Sam leaned down, kissed him and then whispered against his lips. "Protection?" she asked.

"Yes." He did have that. And it wasn't a pathetic box that expired ten years ago, either. He'd ordered a new box of condoms online this week when he was feeling optimistic. He rolled onto his side and moved higher up the bed to reach for the nightstand beside it. He pulled one out and rolled onto his back.

Sam took the foil packet from him and opened it. He gritted his teeth as she sheathed him in latex and crawled back up to him. He could feel his arousal pressing against her inner thigh. She reached between them and aligned their bodies just right. Sam moved his hands back to her hips. And then she nodded.

It was time. He pressed her back, feeling her body slowly expand and envelop him. Inch by inch, he sank into the heat of her until he was fully buried. It was excruciating, balancing the fine line of pleasure as he fought to keep control. He'd waited a long time to finally experience this moment. He wasn't about to let it go by in a flash.

And then Sam started moving her hips. She rocked forward, then back in one long, slow stroke. Brody groaned and pressed his fingertips into the ample flesh of her backside. Sam moved again, this time faster. And again. And again.

She arched her back, giving him a magnificent view of her breasts as she braced herself on his thighs. He moved one hand to slide across her taut stomach and cup a breast. Brody pinched her nipple between his thumb and forefinger, and Sam cried out. She moved faster, thrusting him inside her body at a pace that neither of them could withstand for long.

And then it happened. He felt Sam's inner muscles tighten around him. Her hips continued to move frantically as her cries grew louder. "Brody!" she cried, over and over until Brody could no longer hear her over his own groans of anticipation. As Sam screamed out the last of her orgasm, he let go. The white-hot sensation of pleasure exploded inside, flowing out of him and into Sam in a throbbing, pulsating wave.

"Yes!" was all he could say. Yes, it was really happening. Yes, he was no longer a virgin. Yes, he had the sexiest woman he'd ever seen in his bed. And finally, yes, he would like to do that again very, very soon.

# Seven

Sam awoke the next morning to a beam of sunlight stretching across her face. She pried one eye open to find herself facing a gloriously sunny morning. The windows of Brody's bedroom faced the eastern horizon. She wasn't quite sure if he liked the view or needed nature's alarm clock to wake up.

She turned her head and found the bed empty beside her. Apparently he just liked the view. She ran her hand over the mattress. His side of the bed wasn't even warm. He'd been up for a while. Then her fingers brushed over something unexpected and soft.

With a yawn, she sat up, tugging the sheets to her chest. Looking down, she saw one of her pink roses beside her. She picked it up and brought it to her nose. It was lovely.

The whole night had been amazing. Sam never expected it would be like that. She had been attracted to him from the very beginning. A part of her was drawn to his dark, brooding personality. She wanted to understand him. To know what kind of secrets had driven him into this self-imposed exile. Sam had worried herself to death thinking this was going to be just like the scenario with Luke. She couldn't have been more wrong, but she never imagined Brody would tell her that he was still a virgin.

It surprised Sam, although in retrospect, it was the missing piece that made everything about Brody make sense. The hesitation in his touch. The awkwardness of being near to her. The charming innocence...

When he confessed to her that he'd never been with a woman before, it was one of the saddest and sexiest things she'd ever heard in her life. She'd never been a man's first before, and it was an amazing turn-on for her. Even her first time had been with an older, more experienced guy. You never forget your first. And she wanted so badly to be that woman for Brody.

But she also wanted to make love to Brody because it was something she could do for him. She couldn't free him from his prison. She might not be able to make him a happier, more open person. But she could give him her body. Sam could tell how much his confession pained him. No man ever wanted to have to say that to a woman. And if nothing else ever happened between them, she would be happy knowing she shared that part of herself and lifted one burden of the many from his shoulders.

Sam inhaled the rose's perfume again and flopped back against the pillows. Her muscles ached and she'd barely gotten five hours of sleep, but she didn't care. She was too happy and satiated to care.

The first time they made love, Sam had wanted to

make it all about Brody. Every move, from the seductive slide of her panties over her hips to the glide of her tongue along his aching flesh, had been to give him an experience he would always remember. She took control so he didn't have to worry about making a misstep. Sam had been with more experienced men that fumbled with bra clasps and poked around her body like they were lost. She didn't want that on his mind for even a moment, and it had gone perfectly.

As had everything else last night. By the time they finally fell asleep, no part of her was left unadored, no need unfulfilled.

Sam sighed. A week ago, you couldn't have convinced her that she would be where she was right now. Her irritable mystery boss held more surprises than she ever could've imagined when she first sat at her desk and looked up at those surveillance cameras.

"Sam? Are you awake?"

Before she could answer, Chris leaped up onto the bed and gave her a wet morning kiss on the cheek. Brody scolded her and forced her down off the bed.

Sam sat up, clutching the sheets to her chest. "I am."

Brody gave her a crooked smile of concern. "Were you awake before Mauling 2.0?"

She laughed. "I was. Thank you for my rose."

"You're welcome."

Sam couldn't help but notice how handsome Brody looked this morning. He was wearing a pair of khakis with a white, collared shirt that was rolled up over the muscles of his forearms.

It made her realize what a mess she must be herself. She certainly had bed head, last night's makeup smeared around, and clothes in so many different places she might never find them all to go home today. She ran a self-conscious hand over the wild curls of her hair, but there was nothing her hand could do to tame them. On the bright side, she had a toothbrush in her purse. After years of teenage orthodontia, carrying one with her became a habit she hadn't broken.

"I put your clothes on the chair." Brody pointed to an upholstered chair a few feet away. Each piece of her clothing was neatly folded and stacked there, with her heels on the floor beside it.

"Thank you."

"If you would like to take a shower, there's fresh towels on the stand beside it. I'll be downstairs when you're ready. I was thinking of making breakfast if you're hungry."

"Breakfast?" After last night, she doubted he would attempt cooking again anytime soon.

"Bagels," he corrected with a grin. "I can manage bagels." Brody called Chris and the two of them slipped out of the bedroom, shutting the door behind them.

At least there would be no walk of shame. Sam always hated that part. She flipped back the covers and carried her clothes with her into the master bathroom. The shower stall itself was bigger than her whole bathroom with glass tiles and shiny chrome fixtures. It took her five minutes to figure out which knobs controlled what, but once she got it working, she was rewarded with a decadently hot, steamy spray from three different nozzles.

About thirty minutes later Sam came downstairs. She was a little overdressed, but cleaned up pretty well. She found Brody back in the kitchen. He was pouring two mugs of coffee. She watched him add a splash a cream and a teaspoon of raw sugar before stirring and handing it to her.

"Are my coffee preferences online, too?" she asked.

"Not that I'm aware of." Brody laughed. "But the barista writes it on your cup."

"Oh." Sam took a sip and watched him doctor his own coffee. "So you mentioned bagels?"

"Yes. I have whole wheat, cinnamon raisin and everything."

"Cinnamon raisin would be great." She didn't need poppy seeds in her teeth or onion breath.

"An excellent selection, ma'am. I will toast it to perfection and deliver it to you on the patio if you'd care to relax outside."

"Why, thank you. That would be lovely. Come on, Chris." The dog picked up her red ball and trotted down the hallway with Sam.

This time, Sam paid more attention as she walked through the house. A portrait on the wall caught her eye and she stopped to look at it. There were five people in the portrait, four men and one woman. They all looked like they were in their twenties, each with a different look about them. Brody was in the portrait, smiling, with his arm around the blonde woman. There were pine trees and a bright blue sky behind them.

It was interesting to see Brody like that. He looked so comfortable. He didn't even appear to mind having his picture taken. It was a huge departure from the man she was getting to know. It made her wonder who those people were. And although she had no reason to be jealous considering everything that happened last night, it especially made her wonder who the blonde he hugged to his side was.

Chris waited impatiently for her on the patio. She dropped her ball and barked. Sam continued outside as requested. "Sorry, Chris." She bent down and picked up the ball, tossing it out into the yard.

Chris leaped off the patio, dashing through the dewy morning grass. When she returned, Sam was sitting in the chair by the fireplace. They tossed the ball a few times before Brody showed up with bagels and cream cheese.

"That picture in the hallway," Sam said, after smearing her bagel with the fluffy white cheese. "Who's in it with you? Are they friends from college or something?"

Brody glanced through the doorway and shook his head. "No. That's my family."

His family? Only two out of the five in the portrait shared even the slightest resemblance. She expected Brody to elaborate, but he took a bite of his bagel instead. He didn't seem to want to talk about it. Things had gone well enough that she didn't want to push it. But it made her curious. He never mentioned having brothers and a sister before.

"Are you busy tonight?"

Brody's question startled Sam from her thoughts. "Tonight? No. Why?" She'd already spent a large portion of the weekend with him. She didn't mind seeing him again, but she thought he might be ready for some alone time.

"I still feel bad about dinner last night. I promised you a proper dinner date, and if you're available this evening, I'd like to make good on it."

Sam wrinkled her nose. "Are you attempting to cook again?"

"Oh, no," he said. "This time I'm leaving it up to the professionals."

Brody dialed Sam's phone number at exactly seven that evening. He would've liked to pick her up at her door, but since she lived in a large and busy apartment building, he would have to settle for meeting her at the curb in his Mercedes.

Sam slipped into his passenger seat wearing a pale pink iridescent dress. It was one-shouldered, short and gathered at the waist with a belt made of large chunky rhinestones. When she sat beside him, the dress rode high up her thighs and made her legs look like they went on for miles.

He eyed her with a sly smile. "I told you I was taking you out for dinner, and you wear a dress that makes me want to take you home and strip you naked right now."

Sam grinned. "Do you like it? It's one of my favorites."

"It's very sparkly," he noted.

"It is. And as for stripping me naked, it's all part of the anticipation."

"I've had thirty years of anticipation. It's not novel for me. I'm frankly tired of it."

"Too bad. You said you were taking me to dinner and you're not getting out of it."

Brody reluctantly shifted the car into gear and pulled out of the parking lot. "If you insist."

"Where are we going, anyway? You said you don't go out to eat."

"I don't," he said, ignoring her first question. He wanted to surprise her.

A short while later, they stopped outside of a Beacon Hill town house, the home of one of the finest French and Italian fusion restaurants in Boston. Instead of pulling up to the valet, Brody drove around back and entered a private parking lot.

"Are we really going into a restaurant?" Sam asked. "With people in it?"

"Not exactly." Brody had made special arrangements for a private service. He'd done this once before when Wade brought Tori to Boston, and it had worked out well. He opened the back door and she stepped inside ahead of him. "Take the first right," he said.

Sam turned down the first hallway and they went through a door marked "PRIVATE." The room beyond it was small. At most it could seat four people. A crescent-shaped table extended from the wall. It was draped in white linens and lit with several candles. There were two place settings and two chairs waiting for them.

Brody helped her into her chair at the table and took his own seat. The wall they were facing had a small window with what looked like wooden shutters over it. He reached forward and tapped at the blinds. Less than a minute later, the doors opened and someone reached through to place two glasses of white wine on the table.

"What is this place?" Sam asked. "Are there no menus? No waiters?"

"This restaurant does private chef's tastings. Small groups are invited back here to eat some of the best food in the city. They only take one reservation a night. It's as close as you can get to the action without eating in the kitchen itself. I think you'll like it."

"No one is going to come in the room?"

"Not if they want my generous tip. The only person we will see is the chef. The executive chef presents the food and talks with the diners about what he's prepared."

"Can the chef see us?"

"Yes," Brody said. "But I'm not worried about it. The room is dark enough. He's only going to be interested in what he's serving us."

Sam smiled and sipped her wine. "I was wondering how you would pull this off."

"I thought about renting out an entire restaurant, but this seemed more…intimate." Brody took advantage of the dim lighting and private room to lean in and press his lips against Sam's neck.

She sighed and tipped her head to the side to give him better access. "It certainly has its benefits," she said.

The window opened again and Brody pulled away. The executive chef leaned through the opening and presented them both with a salmon plate with dill and caviar, the first of several courses. Each plate included a perfectly paired wine. It took nearly two hours to complete the tasting, but Brody enjoyed every minute of it. Because Sam did.

He liked watching her face light with excitement as each new course came out. There were a few things she'd never had before, but she was brave enough to try everything and enjoyed almost all of it. Brody ran the risk of some people seeing him while he was here, but it was worth it.

Sam deserved a decadent night out and more. She had changed his entire world since he met her. And last night had been one of the most incredible nights of his life. He'd dreamed of that moment since he was fifteen years old, and nothing he'd imagined in all that time could compare with the reality.

She did everything in her power to make that night special for him. There was no way he could ever repay her for that. But he would try. If everything fell into place the way he hoped, he had a special surprise in store for her.

The chef served their last course and thanked them

for joining him. Brody shook his hand and passed him a credit card to cover dinner and gratuity. They were now left alone to enjoy their trio of canneles. He took his first bite, letting the hazelnut cream melt on his tongue. A moment later, he felt Sam's hand on his thigh.

It seemed as though Sam had a special surprise in store for him, too. He had difficulty swallowing his next bite as her fingers kneaded the muscles, inching ever higher. Brody looked over at Sam. To see her sitting there, she was quietly eating her dessert. If anyone were to see them, they would never suspect that her hand had dipped into his lap.

"Mmm…" she said. She turned to him with a smile and licked the last of the ice cream from her spoon. "The brown butter one is really good." Her dark eyes fixed on him, the elegant line of her brow arching up. "So, do you like it, Brody?"

He knew she wasn't talking about ice cream. "Oh, yeah," he said, nearly groaning as she stroked him through the fabric of his pants. "I think this is the best course so far."

"Me, too." Sam leaned over and kissed him.

Brody dropped his spoon and turned toward her to cup her face in his hands. He really enjoyed kissing Sam. There was something about it that made him want to indulge in kissing her for hours. He didn't know if it was the softness of her lips, the sweet taste of her mouth or the soft cries of desire against his skin, but he couldn't get enough of her.

His hand went to her waist, stroking and clutching at the shimmery fabric of her dress and the skin beneath it. He could think of a few other places he would prefer to touch, but since making love to Sam in this tiny room was not a viable option, he needed to leave the naughty antics to her.

His tongue glided along hers and Sam mimicked the stroke with her hand. Despite the layers of clothing between them, she had him balancing on the edge. He groaned aloud this time, unable to suppress it. Brody was certain someone in the kitchen had heard.

Sam pulled away from him with a smug expression. "What's the matter? Aren't you going to finish your dessert?"

Brody shook his head and grasped Sam's roaming hand with his own. He pulled her away, as much as he hated to do it. "I think I'd like my dessert to go."

# Eight

Sam didn't regret a moment of her weekend, but at the same time, she dreaded this first day back at the office. Would things be weird between them because they had had sex? Would he act differently around her? Or worse yet, would he find a reason to replace her now that he had got what he wanted?

The thoughts haunted her on her Monday morning commute. Her strategy today was to keep quiet, lie low, make Brody come to her and see how he acted around her. She was probably worried over nothing. Things on Sunday morning had been fine. Their dinner was wonderful and dessert was amazing. It wasn't awkward at all. But that didn't mean something else couldn't happen to ruin it.

Sam quietly crept into the office when she arrived. The lights were on, which meant Brody was already in, but his office door was closed. She wasn't quite sure why she was bothering to sneak around. If Brody wanted to know if she was in, he would watch the cameras for her.

She made her way to her desk and found another fresh pink rose in the silver bud vase. Despite her anxiety, the single rose made her smile. It was romantic and sweet, and knowing now that Brody grew the rose himself made it all the more special. After getting to know Brody better this weekend, it was just the kind of thing she would expect from him.

Sam slid the rose to the corner of her desk and busied herself settling in and catching up, but after an hour with no word from Brody in person or via email, she began to worry again.

Somehow, she thought he'd come out to greet her. Or at least ask her for something. He usually buzzed her phone or sent her an instant message once an hour or so. And he'd made a point to always tell her good morning. But today, silence.

The rose was the only thing keeping her from going crazy with anxiety. She opted to focus on her work and try not to worry. He might be busy. His calendar looked open, but he might need to deal with personal matters. Sam had been to his home and taken his virginity, but she really knew very little about Brody's past or his family. He didn't talk about it aside from a few vague comments during dinner Saturday night. He wouldn't have even brought up his family on Sunday morning if Sam hadn't asked him about the picture. And even then, he immediately clammed up about it.

Even as secretive as Brody was, that struck her as odd. He obviously had family. They helped shape who you are as an adult. It was something that came up in conversation. But not once had she heard him mention something funny a brother had done or tell an interesting story about his family. His mother was a bad cook and his father would get angry about it. That small tidbit was enough to make Sam worry that he didn't have the happiest of childhoods, even without his accident.

He hadn't spoken about that, either. The expression on his face as she slipped off his shirt nearly broke her heart. It was so hard for him to expose himself to her like that. It seemed almost painful. And when she saw how far his scars extended across his chest and back, she was surprised and concerned. It was as though a rain of fire had poured down his body.

In addition to that, there were other scars of different types sprinkled across his chest and arms. Small circles, long gashes, deep welts. She hadn't allowed herself to react to the sight of them because he was so self-conscious, but she was still concerned about the scars. What could've caused all these injuries? She couldn't imagine an accident that could do all of this at once. To her, it looked like the results of years of painful abuse.

How long had it taken him to recover from all those injuries?

Sam looked over at the heavy, closed door to his office. Maybe he hadn't recovered at all. Just physically.

Finally, a chime sounded at Sam's computer. She looked down to see an email in her inbox from Brody. It was a forwarded message. His instructions were for her to print the attachments out on the color printer and bring them to him.

Sam scrolled down to the forwarded email. It was from a man named Mickey who worked at Top Secret Private Investigators. The note was brief in the email.

Hey, Brody. Here's what you asked for. Nothing newsworthy on this one. Didn't I run a background check on a secretary for you a few weeks ago? You're going through them like tissue paper, man. Hope this one works out better for you. Let me know if you need anything else.

Sam's stomach sank. Attached to the email was a background investigation on a woman named Deborah Wilder. From Mickey's message, it sounded like this Deborah woman was her replacement. Because despite what he told her Saturday night, he was going to use her and toss her away like Luke had.

Tears stung Sam's eyes as she opened the file and pressed the button to print the paper work as requested. The first page had a picture of the woman. She was thirtysomething with dark hair and a round face. A little chubby. Not particularly attractive, but not unattractive, either. DMV photos were never the most flattering.

Sam's hands were shaking as she picked the pages up off the printer. Looking into the brown eyes of her replacement fueled a fire in her stomach that turned her tears into anger. How dare he ask her to print out the information on her replacement! Was that his way of breaking the news to her? He couldn't even tell her face-to-face?

She snatched the last page of the background check off the machine and pivoted on her heel toward his office. She slung the heavy door open, sending it banging against the wall and swinging back.

Brody stood up, startled, when he heard the racket. His smile of greeting immediately faded into a concerned frown when he saw the furious expression on Sam's face.

"What the hell is this?" she asked, holding the pages up. "Is this how you planned to get rid of me? You can't even tell me to my face?"

The lines of confusion in Brody's forehead deepened as she spoke. Then his gaze darted to the papers in her hand and the photograph of Deborah Wilder on top. "Now, hold on," he began, but Sam didn't listen.

"You know, I believed you when you said you wouldn't sleep with me and toss me aside. Ignorant of me, right? Stupid, trusting Samantha always believes what men tell her."

"Just stop!" Brody yelled over her tirade.

Sam quieted down, but she was far from calm. Her heart was pounding, and her cheeks were hot and flush.

Brody turned to his computer and swore at the screen. "I forwarded you the wrong message," he explained. "I wanted you to print out the quarterly financial reports."

That didn't make Sam feel any better. "So you're still replacing me, but you didn't want me to know yet. Nice."

"No," he insisted. "You're not being fired. Or replaced. I don't want you to go anywhere, Sam. Why would you think I would do that to you after everything that happened between us?"

Sam straightened the paperwork in her hand and started reading Mickey's words back to him. *"You're going through them like tissue paper, man. Hope this one works out better for you."*

"I can explain that," he said.

Sam planted her hands on her hips. "Great. I can't wait to hear it."

"Mickey is the guy I use for background investigations. I hired him to check on you. When I needed some information on someone else, it was easier for me to tell him it was for another secretary. I couldn't tell him the truth."

"Why not?"

Brody frowned at her and took a deep breath before he spoke. "I needed to protect my brother."

"Is this one of the brothers from that picture?" she asked.

"Yes. I have three brothers and a sister. All of us were in that photo you saw in the hallway. My brother Xander is a Congressman. He's been seeing that woman for a few weeks. They've kept it quiet, but he's getting fairly serious about her. I wanted to make sure she didn't have anything in her background that could hurt his reputation and chances of reelection next term."

"You're only investigating your brother's girlfriend?" Sam immediately felt sheepish. The anger and hurt that had rushed through her just a moment ago spiraled away, leaving a hollow place in her chest. She had thrown a hissy fit for no reason.

"Yes."

"And you're not replacing me?"

Brody came out from behind his desk. He took the papers from her hand and set them aside before wrapping his arms around her. "How could I possibly do that?" he asked, hugging her tightly against his chest.

Sam sighed and snuggled against him. "I'm sorry," she said. "I overreacted. This weekend was so nice. It was almost too nice."

"You've been burned before, Sam. That's hard to forget. It's difficult to believe people when they tell you they would never hurt you like that. They have to prove themselves, but even then, a part of you just waits for the other shoe to drop. Believe me, I know all about that."

Sam felt the truth in his words. He'd lived that and his scars were more than only physical ones. She should know better than to think he would do that to her. She hugged him tighter, trying to stave off the tears that threatened again for a different reason.

After a few moments, Brody pulled away. He looked down at her with his hands gently rubbing her upper arms through her sweater. "How does my calendar look at the end of this week?"

Sam shrugged. She hadn't looked this morning. "I'm not sure. Last I checked, you were pretty open."

"Good. And what about you? Do you have any personal plans, say, Wednesday through Sunday?"

Sam didn't have many plans. The past few months of unemployment had put a massive dent in her social life. Even Amanda could barely lure her out of her apartment. "Nothing I know of."

"All right. Today, I want you to clear my calendar of anything this week from Wednesday on. If it's important, move it to Tuesday or next week. And Wednesday morning, I want you to be ready with a suitcase packed for a long weekend. I'll come by your place to pick you up at eight."

Sam's eyes widened with surprise. He was taking her somewhere? Her heart started to flutter with excitement for a moment, but reality quickly set in. The logistics of travel with Brody would be complicated. They'd have to drive and stay in a private residence because anything else would require a hotel or an airplane. Someone would see him. Right? "Where are we going?" she asked.

Brody smiled and shook his head. "It's a surprise."

"And how will I know what I should pack?"

"Dress for warm weather. Very casual. Bring a

swimsuit or two. That should be all you need. If I have things my way, you'll be naked most of the time, anyhow."

He leaned down to kiss her. Sam felt a thrill run down her spine when his lips touched hers. A rush of excitement and arousal pumped through her veins as she molded her body against his.

"Okay," he said, finally pulling away. "That's about all I can handle of that right now, or I'm going to bend you over the pinball machine."

Sam smiled and reluctantly stepped back. "If you insist." She eyed the pinball machine for a moment but opted against pushing him. At least for today.

Brody watched Sam walk out of his office, admiring her snug curves in the skirt she'd worn today. She had an excellent collection of fitted skirts. They were modest in length, with only a small slit up the back to hint at the creamy flesh of her thigh. But now that he knew what delights were hidden beneath that fabric, he had a whole new appreciation for the seductive sway of her hips.

But after she shut the door, the smile faded from his face and he returned to his computer.

How had he made such a stupid mistake? To send Sam the wrong email? Now he knew what his brothers joked about when they said they had sex on the brain. It was a total distraction. Before their weekend together, he would fantasize about her, and now his mind kept drifting back to their time together. He'd had Sam four times in the past two days. There were plenty of images seared in his mind and they kept leaping into his thoughts without invitation.

This could've been a major problem. Thank goodness he'd managed to come up with the story about Xander's non-existent girlfriend. Normally, he didn't like talking about his family—biological or foster. Brody Eden was a ghost. Part of that was not having a past or giving anyone a way to trace him back to being Brody Butler. The press was always looking for an angle to dig up information on him. But this was more important. Sam was held by the confidentiality agreement, and he'd rather talk about his family than tell her what the email was really about.

Sam had bought it without asking any questions he couldn't answer. Her only concern was that this person was her replacement, and he was able to quell those fears with his tale. Fortunately, she hadn't looked closely enough at the report to notice Deborah was recently married with a new baby and didn't live anywhere near Washington D.C.

He shook his head and forwarded her the quarterly report he'd intended to send the first time. Then he reached for the paperwork Sam brought in.

The papers were a little crinkled from the angry way she'd clutched them, but they would do. He'd been reading over the digital copy when Sam burst into his office. He'd been so engrossed in the material, he hadn't noticed she had arrived for the morning. He would've stepped out to say hello. Ignoring her had probably dumped fuel on the fire.

But it didn't take long to scan the pages and realize he had bigger problems than an angry, sexy secretary.

Finding out the real name of dwilder27 hadn't been hard. An evening at home had traced the IP address and with a little digging, he had the name and address of the account owner. From there, he opted to have Mickey do the legwork. The guy was pretty trustworthy when it came to these things. He'd done a great job finding information on his brother Wade's fiancée, Tori. He'd been very thorough on Sam. And judging by the papers in his hands, Mickey had done just as good a job on Deborah Wilder.

He knew it would be a relative of Tommy's. Who else would look for him after all this time? Finding out it was his only sister was a bigger problem. Some curious, estranged relative might be prone to look up someone on the internet from time to time. But they would let it go if they didn't find what they were looking for fairly easily. Not a sister. A sister would keep digging until she found her brother.

That was an issue. He hadn't mentioned anything to his brothers yet. He didn't want to alarm them if it was nothing. But this was something. They needed to know in case Deborah started sniffing around Cornwall looking for the trail Tommy had left for her to follow.

It should be a dead end. Everyone in town would tell her the story they knew as the truth—Tommy had run away from his foster home right before his eighteenth birthday and was never seen or heard from again. Good riddance, as far as most of them were concerned. He and his brothers were fortunate in that way. If they had to be involved in someone's death, at least it was someone most people wouldn't miss. Tommy had been arrested several times for assault and theft. His own parents couldn't handle him and the state had taken him away. Tommy Wilder was trouble; a kid no one but the Edens would even take in. If anyone could get through to him, it was Molly and Ken. But even they couldn't work their magic on him.

Once he came to the Garden of Eden, he immediately started problems. He'd stolen from Molly's cash drawer at the gift shop. He refused to do his share of chores. He'd gotten in a fight with Wade over that and blackened his eye. And none of the boys liked the way he looked at Julianne, who was only thirteen at the time.

Tommy was a ticking time bomb. If he had made it to his eighteenth birthday and left the farm, he would've ended up in jail. Someone would've gotten hurt or worse.

That's what Brody told himself when he thought about that night. Tommy's death hadn't been deliberate, but it had protected the future victims he hadn't gotten around to yet.

Brody picked up the phone and dialed his brother Wade. Wade had lived in Manhattan for years but recently moved back to Cornwall when his fiancée, Tori, finished building their home. It had been a long process, but they'd moved into their massive dream house at the end of September.

If Deborah Wilder showed up in Cornwall, Wade would be the first in the family to know it.

"Hey, Brody," Wade answered, sounding chipper as usual. After he proposed to Tori and their worries about the body being discovered were put to bed, his older brother had tried to forget about their past. He wanted to focus on his upcoming marriage and building their life together.

Brody hated to ruin the bliss, but Wade had to know what was going on. "Hi, Wade. Do you have a private minute? I need to talk to you about something important."

"Sure," Wade said, a serious tone creeping into his voice. "Tori's working in her office upstairs. I'll step out onto the deck in case she comes out."

Brody could hear the doors open and the wind

against the speaker as Wade moved to the patio with the panoramic view of the valley below. "I've gotten a hit on my search query for Tommy. I did some research and it turns out that it's Tommy's younger sister, Deborah. She's looking for him, Wade."

There was a moment of silence on the phone. Brody had a bad reputation for being the buzzkill of the family, but this couldn't be dismissed as his paranoia.

"What have you found out?" Wade finally responded.

"I got the first hit about a week ago and started looking into the user's information. Since then, she's tried a couple more times with different search strings, but she hasn't had any luck. I'm worried she might come to town and start asking questions. I wanted you to be prepared since you'll likely hear about it first if she does."

"Okay. I'll put a bug in Skippy's ear."

Skippy was the bartender who worked in the local Cornwall watering hole, the Wet Hen. He was a hundred-and-fifty years old if he was a day, with skin like aged leather and hearing like a dog. "Do you really think you can trust Skippy with something like this?"

"Absolutely. Skippy knows everything that goes on in this town. Hell, I wouldn't be surprised if Skippy already knows about Tommy and what happened. He's a bartender. He's paid to listen and not talk. If he wanted to, he could probably blackmail half the county with the things he knows. He wouldn't tell a soul. Besides, if she shows up, odds are, she'll end up at the Hen. I can count on him to let me know the moment she arrives, even if I don't tell him why it's important."

Wade seemed confident in Skippy. Brody was less so, but he would defer to his older brother on this point. "Her name is Deborah Curtis now, although she might still introduce herself as Deborah Wilder if she's talking to people that might have known her or her brother as children. Curtis is her married name. She lives in Hartford with her husband and six-month-old daughter."

"Do you think she's going to be a problem?"

"I don't know," Brody admitted. "If our story sticks, she won't get anywhere asking questions. Everyone will tell her he ran away and she'll go home disappointed."

"You don't think our story will stick? We did a pretty convincing job. Xander burned all of his things. I told Ken and Molly I heard him sneak out in the night. Until there's a body there's no reason for anyone to question it. He could've crossed into Canada on foot and changed his name. There would be no trace of him."

Brody wished he could be as confident as Wade was. "I hope you're right. But keep an eye out for her, just in case."

"I will. I'll let you know the moment I hear something. I've got a question for you on a different subject, though."

Brody frowned at the phone. He didn't like the subtle teasing tone Wade's voice had taken on. "Yes?"

"I spoke with Xander the other day. He mentioned you had a *lady friend*."

Brody couldn't disguise his heavy sigh. If you told one brother, you might as well tell them all. They were worse than gossiping old women sometimes. "You could say that."

"Is it serious?"

"I'm not sure. It's a little early to speculate."

"Why didn't you tell me about her?" Wade complained. "Who is she? Where did you meet her? You don't go anywhere."

"I didn't tell you because there wasn't much to tell at the time. I only mentioned it to Xander so he'd stop trying to fix me up with a plastic surgeon. Anyway, to make a long story short, it's my administrative assistant."

"Agnes?" Wade asked, his voice strained with incredulity.

"No, not Agnes," Brody snapped in irritation. "I'm not so hard up that I'd chase after my married, retirement-age secretary. She's older than Mom, I think."

"Whatever floats your boat, man. I just want to see you with someone."

"That does *not* float my boat. Her name is Samantha. She's filling in for Agnes who is on vacation."

"I remember you saying something about that, but I wasn't sure when she was leaving town. So, it's going *well?*" There was a naughty lilt to the way he spoke that made his real question very clear. Wade didn't know Brody had been a virgin until a few days ago, but even then, he didn't think Brody got nearly enough action for a man in his prime.

"It's going *extremely* well," Brody replied. He couldn't keep the wide grin on his face from slipping into his voice. "She's amazing. Beautiful. Smart. And so sexy I can barely focus on my work."

"Wow," Wade commented. "You're damn near gushing. I hope we'll get to meet her soon. Maybe you can bring her to the farm for Christmas. In the meantime, congratulations for getting laid in this decade, Bro. I feel like we should throw you a party or something."

Brody shook his head and chuckled at his brother's blunt observation. If he only knew the truth....

# Nine

"Are we going to a big city?" Sam attempted to uncover their secret destination for the tenth time today by playing twenty questions. The moment she and Brody loaded up in his car, she'd started in on him. So far, she'd eliminated Dallas, Los Angeles, Orlando and New Orleans. He told her it was someplace she could dress warm and bring a swimsuit. They weren't going to a lake or a river. He hadn't told her to pack her passport, so that eliminated the Caribbean and Mexico.

"No." Brody didn't even look her way when he answered. His eyes were focused on the expressway and the morning traffic.

"Are we going to the beach?"

Brody sighed. "Give it up. I'm not going to tell you."

"We *are* going to the beach," she said. "Otherwise you would've said no. Are we going to the Florida Keys?"

He didn't respond but slowed the car and turned into a private airport outside of the city. They drove past the main terminal to a hangar on the far side of the property. It had a sign on the side that said "Confidential Luxury Private Jets."

Since Brody told her they were taking a trip, she hadn't been able to fathom how they were going to get there when he didn't go out in public. She'd thought perhaps their destination was within driving distance. It never occurred to her that they could take a private jet instead of a regular, commercial airliner. Of course, she couldn't afford a jet in a million years, so she wouldn't have even dreamed of it.

Brody paused outside the hangar and honked his horn in two short bursts and one long one. A moment later, the massive door rolled up to reveal a shiny white jet inside. Brody pulled into the hangar and parked his car in the far corner. He killed the engine but left the keys in the ignition. "Come on," he said with a sly smile. He was enjoying torturing her with this surprise.

They got out of the car and Brody opened the trunk. Instead of pulling out their bags, he took her arm and led her across the empty building to the jet. She expected a place like this to have crew running all over the place. Or at the very least a pilot and someone to direct the plane. "Where are all their employees?" she asked.

"They're hiding inside until we get on the plane."

"Why?"

Brody turned to her with an amused expression. "Because I pay them to, of course."

That made sense. With enough money, Brody could do things however he chose to. It had gotten so easy to look at him and not see the scars any longer. But everyone else still saw them. And Brody was still living a shadow of a life. She started up the stairs of the jet with Brody behind her. The cockpit door to the left was already closed with the pilots inside.

The sign on the building had been right. This was a luxury jet. It didn't look like any plane she'd ever been inside. It had plush gray carpeting and captain's chairs that faced each other with polished mahogany tables between them. A large flat screen television was mounted on the far rear wall with a row of seats that turned to face it. There was a minibar, a sofa, a dining room table and what looked like a full-size bed in a room beyond the television. A bucket of ice with a bottle of champagne was waiting on the table beside them as they entered.

"Wow," was all Sam could say. And to think she thought flying first class was something special.

Brody pulled a thick curtain to separate them from the front of the plane. Sam settled into one of the soft leather seats as the engine of the plane roared to life. Someone she couldn't see came out of the cockpit to close and secure the door and then disappeared back inside.

She looked out the window to see ten employees appear out of nowhere. Several loaded their bags into the cargo hold. Others were using neon batons to guide the plane out of the hangar and toward the runway.

Brody sat down beside her with a flute of champagne in each hand. "Here you go."

Sam accepted one and took a sip. The golden bubbles exploded on her tongue with a seductively smooth, dry flavor. It was really nice champagne. Nothing like the sparkling wine she bought at the grocery store on New Year's Eve.

"Time to buckle up," Brody said with a smile.

The plane slowly taxied down the winding paths of the small airport. Sam could only watch in amazement.

"Good morning, Mr. Eden," a man's voice announced through the overhead speaker. "We'd like to welcome you and Ms. Davis aboard our luxury jet today. I am your Captain, Louis Holmes, and my co-pilot is Rene Lejeune. Please let us know by pressing the call button if there is anything we can do for you. We are currently number two for take-off. Our flight time today will be about four hours, and we have smooth, clear skies ahead of us. As requested, a prepared brunch is waiting for you in the dining area. The seat belt sign will turn off when we've reached cruising altitude and it's safe for you to move about the cabin. Enjoy your flight."

Sam took another sip of her champagne and blinked a few times to see if her amazing surroundings would disappear. "Is this how you usually travel? I can't even imagine this being the norm."

Brody nodded. "If it's too far to drive, yes. I have standing orders with this company and they know exactly how I want things arranged. Normally there would be a flight attendant that would bring us drinks and serve us lunch, but I decline her services on my flights for apparent reasons."

"When was the last time you flew on a regular plane?"

Brody thought hard for a second, narrowing his eyes at her as he tried to remember. "I flew with my dad to Ohio when I was sixteen."

"What was in Ohio? Family?"

"No. We went to see a doctor and facility there that specialized in the latest and greatest burn reconstruction procedures. He was the best in the country at the time. We had high hopes that he could help me."

Sam sat silently waiting for him to continue. When he didn't, she prompted, "What happened?"

Brody looked at her, his brow furrowed. "Obviously nothing could be done or I wouldn't look like this."

Sam opted not to press on that topic. Instead, she reached for his hand and held it as the engines kicked into high gear and they started down the runway. She wasn't afraid of flying, but she still got a little nervous, especially in a small plane like this one.

A few minutes later, she was able to look out her window and see nothing but ocean. "This is amazing."

"I'm glad you think so. But you ain't seen nothing yet."

Sam smiled and sank into the plush leather of her seat, thinking she could fall asleep that instant, it was so comfortable. By the time the plane leveled off and the seat belt light kicked off, she had finished her champagne and was fairly certain life didn't get much better than this. "You're going to spoil me with all this luxury. Ten-course meals, private jets... What am I going to do the next time I have to fly coach and eat fast food?"

"Sadly, you'll have to suffer like the other 99.9 percent of the population. Are you hungry?" Brody asked.

"Yes." Sam had forgotten her protein bar when they left this morning, and her stomach had been rumbling for a while. The champagne went straight to her head on an empty stomach.

"Let's go check out what they left us for brunch."

Sam followed him back to the dining area. On top of the minibar was a platter with all sorts of breads and pastries. In the refrigerator was an assortment of sliced fruits, cheeses and rolled, thin sliced deli meats. There was a plate of canapés like bellinis with caviar and crème fraiche and another with a fresh variety of

sushi. Two pitchers were in the bottom of the refrigerator. One hold a dark red sangria and the other, a cold
strawberry mint soup.

It was more than she could eat in a few days, much
less a few hours.

"I hope you skipped breakfast," Brody said, pulling
the first platters out to sit on the dining table.

"I guess I'll eat myself into a coma and then go flop
onto the bed in the back." Sam scooped up the tray of
baked goods and followed him.

"That sounds like an excellent plan." Brody held out
a strawberry to Sam and she took a bite of the juicy
fruit. "Ever considered joining the Mile High Club?"

Several hours later, they touched down on the small
island of Culebra, Puerto Rico. Brody watched Sam
gaze out the window at everything as they taxied
through the small airport. When they got off the jet, a
limo was waiting for them. The driver did not get out
of the car to greet them as they usually did. Instead,
Brody opened the door for both of them to climb inside.
The partition between the front and back of the limo
was closed. He could hear the driver's door open once
they were in the car. Through the dark-tinted glass, Sam
watched the driver collect their bags from the jet and
place them in the trunk.

"So, are we staying in Puerto Rico?" she asked.

"Nope." He has having fun playing this game with
her. She couldn't stand not knowing what was going on.

"And where are we going from here?"

"To the marina."

"We're going on a boat?"

Brody turned in the plush leather seat to look at her.
Sam's cheeks were still a touch flush and her hair a bit

disheveled from their private tumble in the back of the plane. Every time he flew down here, he'd eyed the jet's bed and fantasized about using it for more than a nap. Given that he always flew alone, it wasn't really a possibility until now. "You aren't good with surprises, are you?"

She shrugged, a sheepish look drawing down her smile. "No, sorry."

Brody put his arm around her shoulder and sidled up alongside her. He kissed her temple and whispered into her ear. "Why don't you just enjoy the trip and I'll let you know when we're at our final destination?"

The limo started to pull away as she reluctantly agreed. There wasn't long to wait. The car arrived at the marina only a few minutes after leaving the airport property. After the driver moved their luggage to the deck of a small speedboat, they got out. The car pulled away as Brody helped Sam down onto the deck. He'd made enough trips out here and paid enough money that everyone had his requested process down pat.

Brody started up the boat and slowly chartered it out of the marina and into the open water. Sam sat beside him, marveling at the view. The water here was amazing—bright turquoise, clear and sparkling. You could see the schools of fish moving through the water beside them. The sky was a vivid blue without a single cloud to mar it. It was a beautiful day to be in the Caribbean.

After about thirty minutes of plowing into the open water toward his desired coordinates, Brody spied the dark shape of their destination on the horizon. "We're almost there," he said.

Sam watched anxiously as the island came into view. He couldn't tell Sam where they were going because the island technically didn't have a name. He hadn't gone to the trouble of officially naming it yet. When he purchased the island, he was told a few of the locals called it *Joya Verde,* Green Jewel, but it wasn't plotted as such on any maps.

Brody slowed the boat as they reached more shallow waters and pulled up alongside the dock that stretched out into the water from the beach. He tied up the boat, hauled their bags onto the pier and helped Sam out.

The look on her face was priceless. It was half the reason he wanted to bring her here. Her eyes were wide, her mouth open, as she took in every sight. He had reacted the same way when he first saw his green jewel. It was a beautiful little island with smooth golden sand beaches, dark green palms and other lush plants that grew out of the jutting black rock. There was about six acres of the island to explore while they were here. Around the other side was a mangrove lagoon that harbored a surprise he would show Sam later.

"What is this place?" she asked.

"It's my escape. The only place in the whole world where I can walk on the beach or swim in the ocean without the prying eyes of another living soul on me."

Sam had started rolling her suitcase toward the beach but stopped and turned to him. "You own an island? The whole thing?"

"Yes. It seemed like a good investment since I can't travel anywhere else."

Sam shook her head and continued on her path to the shore. "Rich people," she muttered under her breath.

Brody laughed at her and led the way from the beach up a winding path to the house that was made of crushed seashells and small pebbles. He opened the front door of the two-story beach house and gestured her in ahead of him. He hadn't built the home, but he was eternally grateful to the previous owner who had. The house was built on the edge of a rocky incline that rose up from the beach. The entire front of the home facing the ocean was glass, floor to ceiling. It faced west, so he could watch the sunset every night.

The floor plan was open and modern. The first floor had a gourmet kitchen, a great room and a deck with a swimming pool, hot tub and an outdoor shower. Off of the deck were stairs leading down to the beach. The entire second floor was dedicated to the master suite. This was not a vacation home for families. There was only the one bedroom. This was a retreat for lovers, or more appropriately, millionaire recluses.

"Come upstairs and I'll show you the best part."

Sam followed him up a winding open staircase to the master bedroom. Directly over the bed was a massive, square skylight that made you feel like you were sleeping beneath the stars. He'd lain there many nights, counting them until he fell asleep. Last, he led her out onto the second-story balcony. It wrapped around three sides of the house. The breeze was a little cooler up here, especially in the winter, but the view was exquisite.

She walked out to the railing and Brody came up behind her. She leaned back and he wrapped his arms around her waist to pull her tight against him. They looked out together at the vast aqua ocean that sprawled ahead of them. It was a patchwork of various shades of blue and green as the water changed depths and covered coral reefs. In the distance, they could see the faint outline of Culebra, but it was the only thing in sight.

"Not a bad view, eh?"

"It's so beautiful," she breathed. "I've never seen anything like it."

"It's not nearly as beautiful as you are."

Sam turned in his arms until she was facing him. She reached up and pulled the sunglasses from his face. "I want to be able to see those gorgeous baby blues."

Brody tried not to chuckle bitterly at her compliment, but he couldn't help it. He didn't see anything about himself as attractive. He'd never liked his eyes. They were exactly like his father's. When he looked in the mirror, all he could see was his father's dark, angry, blue gaze fixed on him when he did something wrong. And as for the parts of his face he did like, his father had ruined that, as well.

"What's so funny?" Sam asked, wrinkling her nose with irritation.

"Nothing is funny. I just have no idea what it is about me that you're attracted to," he admitted.

"Everyone has flaws. I hate my nose," Sam complained. "I took a soccer ball to the face when I was nine and it's bothered me ever since then. It didn't heal right. I also have troll feet, so I wear cute shoes to disguise them. I won't even get started on my hips."

"You have excellent hips."

"Thank you, but I've never been happy with them. I jog constantly, but there they stay. The point is that you are always going to be your own biggest critic. But everyone has at least one attractive feature. The key is to make the most of your best features. At the wrong angle my nose might make me look like I've lost a boxing match, but when I'm having a good hair day, I feel great about myself. The more confident you are, the more attractive you appear to others."

That was a nice idea. And given that Sam was nitpicking her minor imperfections, that might work for her. But if he had to see beauty in himself for others to see it, he was doomed. He shook his head and looked back at the horizon. He was uncomfortable with the way she was studying him. Even knowing that for some unfathomable reason she was attracted to him, he wanted to squirm under her gaze.

"Look at me, Brody." Her hand rested against his scarred cheek and turned his face back to her. "You don't see anything but the scars, do you?"

He swallowed hard but couldn't avoid her question. "I do. Usually the scars are the last thing I notice. Mostly, I see the drunk, angry face of my father. Sometimes I see my mother's mouth, tight with disapproval and stone-silent when child protective services asked her questions. But the worst is when I see how I used to look before this happened and what I might look like today if I hadn't startled him that day in the garage."

His words were harsher than he intended them to be, but he needed Sam to understand. There was nothing beautiful about him in his opinion. He was broken.

"What happened to you, Brody?"

He didn't want to talk about it. Not here in this magical place where he could escape from his past. He never should've said the words to lead them to the conversation he dreaded. He should've nodded and accepted her compliment. And yet, he knew he needed to tell her. After sharing something as intimate as they had, she deserved to know why he was the way he was. That didn't mean he had to like it.

Brody's hands dropped from Sam's waist and he turned to walk back into the house. He heard her come in behind him and slide the glass door closed.

"Brody, please."

He sank onto the edge of the bed and dropped his head to look down at the polished wood floors between his feet. The bed sagged as Sam sat beside him. She placed a reassuring hand on his knee.

"My father was the best-looking guy in Goshen, Connecticut. He also had a raging temper and was an alcoholic by the time he was twenty-three. My mother was an enabler with no self-esteem. She always thought she wasn't good enough for a man like him. Probably because he told her she was fat and ugly at every opportunity. Why they got married, I'll never know, but at least they bothered to. My mother thought that having his son would be the best way to win him over."

Sam's sharp intake of breath beside him was enough to let him know she knew it was a bad idea. "What she didn't realize was that any child she had would be just as big a disappointment to him as she was. I could never do anything right. Sometimes I think my father only wore a belt so he would always have something handy to hit me with."

Her hand tightened on his knee, but she didn't speak. "I didn't believe it was possible, but he got meaner as he got older. When the belt didn't make me scream loud enough anymore, he switched to fists. Or burning cigarettes. My mother looked the other way and would lecture me about angering him while she bandaged my wounds. By the time I reached fifth grade, I was certain it was coming down to a final fight. Him versus me. I was finally getting big enough and strong enough to fight back.

"One day I came home from school and he wasn't at work like he should've been. His car had a dead battery, so he was in the garage working on it. I don't know why I went out there that day. I should have just gone into my room and hid like I usually did. When I opened the door, it made a loud squeaking noise and startled him. He hit the back of his head on the hood of the car and dropped the car battery he was pulling out. Somehow, it spilled some of the acid on his hand and he started yelling."

The rest of the day was a sketchy composite of memories and things that people told him. "I remember my father screaming and hitting me. I remember slumping against the wall and sliding to the ground, fighting to stay conscious. I opened my eyes at one point and saw him walking toward me with something in his hand. I tried to shield myself, but it was a pointless effort. After that, I only recall hearing someone screaming and realizing it was me. I blacked out and woke up in the hospital a week later."

"Oh, my God," Sam said.

Brody turned to look at her and saw the tears welling in her eyes. "Please don't cry. I don't want to upset you. This was twenty years ago. It's too late to cry now."

"What was it?" she asked, her voice almost too quiet for him to hear her.

"After he beat me, he poured the acid from his battery into an empty quart-size can we'd recently used to paint the bathroom. Then he threw it at me. The neighbors called the cops when they heard me screaming."

"Please tell me that he's in jail."

"He is, at least for now. If he had stuck with beating me as usual, the maximum sentence in Connecticut is a year, but the prosecutor nailed him with first-degree assault against a minor ten and under and he got twenty years, the maximum sentence. I went into foster care after that."

"What about your mother?"

For some reason, this was the part of the story that always bothered him the most. His father was a bastard. He'd come to terms with that long before the accident. But her... "She chose him."

"She *what?*" Sam's voice was sharp and angry. He wished his mother had shown half as much emotion for him.

"She blamed me for my father going to prison. I brought the worst out in him, you see. To this day, she goes to every parole hearing and begs them to let him out. That's the one public place I do go. The judge usually takes one look at me and sends him right back to the prison. She hates me for that, but it's only fair since I hate her for choosing a man over her child. I might not have gone into foster care, but she never came to the hospital to claim me, so social services had no choice."

"What a horrible mother."

"You'd think so, but it turned out to be the best thing she could've done for me. I would've done nothing with my life if I had stayed with her, but my foster home was amazing. My foster family is my real family now. Wade, Xander and Heath are my brothers. Julianne is my sister. Molly and Ken are my parents. They never looked at me like I was different. They gave me the faith and drive to make something of myself. Without them, I wouldn't have built my company and I certainly wouldn't be flying in jets to my private island. My life is so much better because of the Edens. That's why I took their last name when I turned eighteen. If it weren't for these damn scars, I might even forget that my biological parents ever existed."

Sam sat quietly for a moment, absorbing everything he'd told her. "I'm glad you found people who cared about you, Brody. I can't imagine what you've been through, especially so young. But thank you for sharing this with me. I know that was hard for you."

Brody covered Sam's hand with his own and gave it a gentle squeeze. It was done. He'd put everything out there. And now he wouldn't have to talk about it again. Ever.

Hopefully, now, they could start to enjoy their vacation. "Now that all that unpleasantness is out of the way, what do you say to putting on our swimsuits and taking a dip in that fantastic ocean?"

# Ten

"Where exactly are we going again?" Sam clutched her flashlight and followed Brody down a dim, gravel and sand path.

"I didn't say."

Sam would normally say that she liked surprises, but Brody seemed full of them. She never knew what they were doing. But considering his last surprise included a luxury jet and a private island, she needed to just go with it. They'd spent two days on the island being decadently lazy. After dinner, he'd eyed the darkening sky and told her to put on her swimsuit. She couldn't fathom what she would do in the dark in her swimsuit, especially when he handed her a flashlight.

Walking through the dark to the far side of the island made her even more nervous. The path they traveled was narrow and went straight through his private rain-forest. There were strange trees and potentially poisonous plants and unseen things living in them. She could hear *something* rustling in the branches, but she couldn't find it with her flashlight. Hopefully it was a bird and not some big scary lizard or snake.

"We're almost there," Brody said, rounding a thick, knotted tree trunk. He was clutching a camping lantern in his hand.

The path curved ahead of them and opened to a small oval lagoon ringed with a dark tangle of trees and vines. It was almost entirely enclosed from the ocean except for a narrow inlet. There were no sandy beaches on this part of the island. At least that she could see. By now the sun had fully set and there was only a touch of purple lighting the night sky. There was no moon tonight, but there was enough light left to see two kayaks and paddles lying along their path.

"We're going kayaking?" That wasn't exactly what she had in mind.

"Yes." Brody hung the lantern on a sturdy branch and bent down to pick up a paddle. "Have you ever done it before?"

"No. I'm not particularly outdoorsy."

"That's okay. It isn't hard. The water is calm tonight. These are open kayaks, so you don't have to worry about rolling it."

Sam swallowed hard and eyed him with renewed concern. She hadn't considered *that* until he mentioned it. "Great. Any particular reason why we're doing this in the dark? No one will see us."

"I know. But we have to go in the dark. You'll see why." He grabbed one of the kayaks and hauled it to the edge of the water. "Come here and step in."

Sam made her way over and kicked off her flip flops. Brody braced the kayak and held it steady as she climbed inside and sat down. It rocked slightly, but she kept her balance.

Brody handed her the two-ended paddle. "I'm going to push you off so I can put mine in the water. Just sit still and don't paddle around until I get out there with you."

She braced herself for the push and glided out into the lagoon. A few minutes later Brody pulled up alongside her. "Let's paddle out into the middle. It's almost dark enough."

Sam dipped her paddle into the water on one side of the kayak, then the other. She was surprised at how easily she moved across the surface. It only took a few moments to reach the center of the lagoon. She let the kayak glide to a stop and held her paddle across her lap. The night was silent and still around them. She looked up to the dark sky and gasped. With no sun, moon or city lights, the stars were like a thick blanket overhead. There were millions scattered across the darkness instead of the fifty she was lucky to see in Boston. Suddenly, the mysterious hike through the dark was worth it.

"It's beautiful," she said.

Brody looked up at the sky and laughed. "Yes, it is. But that's not why we're here."

"It's not?"

"No. I wanted to show this place to you. It's a secret. No one knows this is here. I don't even think the previous owner knew. I found it by accident. There are only a few locations like this in the whole world and mine may be the only privately owned one."

Sam looked around herself, searching for what made it so special. She didn't see anything but some weird trees. And then she saw it. A fish darted through the water beside her. It glowed a bluish-white, leaving a streak behind it like a trail of stardust. After a moment it faded away. "What was that?" she asked. "You have glowing fish."

Brody smiled. "It must be dark enough now. It's not the fish that glow. Watch." He dipped his paddle into the water and agitated it. It stirred up a swirl of glowing white clouds beneath the surface.

Sam did the same with her own paddle. Every movement generated the blue glow in the inky black water. It was eerie and hauntingly beautiful. She'd never seen anything like it before. "What makes it do that?"

"This is a bioluminescent bay. The mangrove lagoon and warm, calm water creates the perfect environment for the tiny little creatures to thrive. They put off a blue-green glow as a defense mechanism when they're agitated by movement."

"Is it safe to put my hand in the water?"

"As long as you don't have on any bug repellant. It will kill them."

"I don't." Sam let her fingers comb through the water, making squiggly green designs like she was drawing in the air with sparklers on the Fourth of July. When she pulled her hand out of the water, it glowed for a moment. "Wow. This is really incredible."

"I thought you'd like it. Do you want to get in?"

Sam smiled. "Can we?"

"Yeah." Brody laid his paddle inside the kayak and threw his legs over the side into the water.

Sam watched him slip beneath the surface of the water in a haze of blue-green clouds. She could follow his every movement through the dark water. He swam under her kayak coming up on the opposite side. When

he surfaced, his whole body was dripping with iridescent green water.

"Come on," he said, holding his hand out to her.

She was nervous about swimming in the ocean at
night, but she couldn't pass up this opportunity. She'd
try to forget there might be sharks or other creepy creatures nearby.

Sam took his hand and followed his lead, throwing
her legs over the side and slipping into the water. She
was too nervous to stay under for long and immediately
reached for the surface. When she reopened her eyes,
she was amazed by the glow of her every movement as
she treaded water.

Brody watched her with a soft smile curling his lips.
It was a curious expression considering their circumstances. "What?" she finally asked as she pushed a wet
strand of hair out of her face.

"You're even beautiful when you're green."

Sam chuckled and shook her head. If she looked anything like Brody did, it was more likely that she looked
like a human glow stick or space alien. Of course, Brody
looked handsome even as the drops of luminescent
water dripped down his cheeks. The glow of the water
around them was bright enough for her to see his face
clearly in the darkness. Nothing about him had physically changed, and yet he looked like a completely different person here on his island. It had taken until today
for her to really notice the change, but it was definitely
there. He was relaxed. Open. She dared say he even
looked happy. He didn't have the same countenance in
Boston. Not even at his home, which should've been a
place he could relax and be himself.

It was as though a massive burden had been lifted
from his shoulders coming here. Maybe telling her

about his past and his parents had helped, too. That was a huge secret to carry around. He had his foster family, which was wonderful, but who else could he talk to? Confide in? Not Agnes. But he could tell Sam. And she was glad to be that for him.

As she watched him here, in this beautiful, magical moment, she realized she wanted to be more to him than a confidante. More than just his secretary. Sam wanted to be with Brody. And not only physically. The shy, mysterious charmer had stolen her heart away.

Temporarily stunned by the turn of her thoughts, she stopped swimming and her head slipped under the water again. It was too deep in this part of the lagoon. She pushed herself back up, turned and started swimming closer to the shore where they'd come in. She stopped when she could feel sand and stones scraping against her toes. It made her feel more stable physically, if nothing else. "That's better."

"Was the water too deep?" Brody asked, coming up behind her.

Sam turned to him and smiled. She didn't want him to know she was having thoughts about her feelings for him. "Not usually. But it's so amazing and romantic out here, and I want to kiss you so badly. I'm afraid I'll get distracted touching you and drown."

Brody chuckled, wrapping his arms around her and pulling her against him. She moved easily through the water, colliding with his chest. "I'll keep your head above water, don't worry."

She was sure he would. His hands glided over her bare back. He'd grown so much more confident since that first night. He was a quick learner, she was pleased to discover. Like a true left-brainer, he had set his mind to learning every inch of her body, memorizing every response. She'd never had a man figure out so quickly how she liked to be touched.

When his lips met hers, she felt a chill of excitement run down her spine. With a little hop and a luminescent cloud following her movement, she wrapped her legs around his waist and pressed her body into his. Brody groaned against her mouth as her center made contact with the firm heat of his arousal. The thin fabric of her bikini bottoms and his swimming trunks did little to disguise how badly he wanted her.

Sam was intrigued about the idea of making love to him right here. The blanket of stars and eerie glow of their movements was so romantic. But there were no smooth sandy beaches here. Or protection. It was an interesting but impractical idea. They needed to go back to the house.

"Take me to bed," she whispered.

Brody complied, walking them out of the water and onto the beach. She expected him to put her down once they reached the trail back to the house, but he didn't. He continued walking, carrying her as though she were no heavier than a small child. She clung to him, burying her face in his neck. She couldn't resist tasting his skin with him so close. Her lips and tongue moved over him. He tasted salty from the ocean.

Seeing the lights of the house shining on the landscape around them made her bolder. She let her tongue swirl up the side of his neck to the sensitive skin just below his earlobe. She flicked it and then gently bit at him. She could feel Brody shiver and tighten his grip on her.

They climbed the steps to the deck with the pool and walked through the open sliding glass door. Brody continued up the stairs to the master loft without putting her

down, but she could feel the gentle tug of his fingertips
at the tie of her bikini top. Easing back from her grip on
him, she let the tiny white fabric slide down and fall to
the ground, exposing her breasts and the tight pink tips.

Brody allowed his gaze to dip down for a moment,
then tore it away so he didn't trip on the stairs. Sam
pressed her breasts into his bare chest, eliciting a sharp
hiss in her ear.

At the top of the stairs, he went directly to the bed,
dropping her onto the mattress and immediately covering her body with his own. Sam was grateful for the
heat of him over her. The cooler air of the house combined with her still damp hair and skin drew goose
bumps across her flesh and made her nipples even more
painfully tight. Brody captured one in his mouth, and
the sharp pleasure of it sent her head flying back with
a gasp.

It was then that she saw that they'd brought the blanket of stars back to the house with them. The skylight
over the bed showed a perfect snapshot of the inky
black night with its shimmering sea of twinkling stars
overhead. It was awe-inspiring, and combined with the
pleasure of Brody's hands gliding over her skin, she was
very nearly overwhelmed by the moment.

Everything about the past few days had been perfect.
Like a dream she never even dared to imagine. Even
Brody's confession about his childhood, while tragic,
had breached one of the last barriers between them.
She'd never felt closer to another man in her life. He
was amazing in so many different ways and he didn't
even know it.

She wished she knew of a way to tell him that he
would believe. Words were easily brushed off. She

would have to show him how much he meant to her. How much she…loved him.

Sam tried to take a deep breath and focus on the stars overhead as tears started to form in the corners of her eyes. Her chest was painfully tight, even as her stomach fluttered with excitement and nerves.

"Sam, is something wrong?"

She shifted her gaze from the skylight to Brody's concerned face. He was hovering over her, his strong arms pressed into the mattress beside her. His damp hair was curling slightly as it dried, and his eyes were black in the dim light but still just as penetrating. He was worried that he'd done something wrong, when in fact, he'd done everything right.

At that exact moment, the first tear rolled down the side of her face. With a slight shake of her head and a soft smile, she reached out and pulled him back down to her. She closed her eyes as their lips met and another tear escaped. She wasn't certain if most men understood tears of emotions other than pain and sadness. Sam could cry through any number of emotions, including joy and contentedness. And she was anything but sad right now. Being with Brody here on this beautiful island felt so perfectly right.

When he eased forward and filled her, she could only cling to him and bite her bottom lip to keep from telling him how she felt. It would be so easy to whisper it into his ear or to cry it out to the night when she came undone. But she was afraid to. There was no way to know how he would react, and she didn't dare ruin this moment. There would be time later, and maybe then, she might get the response she wanted to hear.

Instead, she turned off her thoughts and tried to focus on loving him. It wasn't long before she was swept up in the pleasure he coaxed from her, drunk on the warm musk of his skin. When her powerful climax came, she didn't cry out. She buried her face in his neck, gasping his name as he filled her again and again.

Brody was tossing the last of his things in his suitcase when his cell phone rang. It was Wade's ringtone, "Opportunities" by the Pet Shop Boys. The song was upbeat, but for some reason, it made his stomach ache with dread. Wade knew he was at the island with Sam. He would only call if it was really important.

Deborah Wilder.

He checked to make sure Sam was still in the shower before he answered the phone. "Hello?"

"I'm sorry to interrupt your trip," Wade began, but Brody could tell exactly where this was going. "You told me to call the minute I heard something."

Brody sank down onto the bed and let Wade talk without interruption.

"Deborah is in Cornwall. She was at the Wet Hen last night asking around for anyone that knew her brother."

The Wet Hen was the center for a lot of activity in their home town. If you wanted to have a beer with the mayor and the sheriff, that was the place to go. It was also the place to start trouble quickly because everyone in town would know about it as certainly as they were sitting there.

"Skippy called, but by the time I got down to the bar, she was gone. I hung around and chatted with a few folks for a while. It didn't take much to find out what happened before she left."

"Did she learn anything?"

"No," Wade said. "It's been a long time and most people have forgotten Tommy Wilder even existed. Those that remembered told her what she already knew—he ran away from his foster home and was never seen in Cornwall again."

Brody nodded. Maybe that would be enough to convince her that Cornwall was a dead end and send her packing. "Is she still in town?"

"Yes. And apparently she went to the farm first to talk to Mom and Dad."

"What?" Brody nearly shouted into the phone. This was way too close for comfort.

"I didn't find out until later. Mom mentioned it when I went by this morning. Nothing came of it, but Mom is a little upset to know that Tommy has been missing since the night he vanished. I don't think she's ever forgiven herself for 'failing' that one."

Even knowing that she'd raised three millionaire CEOs, a U.S. congressman and a world-acclaimed artist, Molly would focus on the one that got away. "Not even Mom could have saved Tommy. I hate that she upset Mom like that. Where is Deborah staying?"

"She's staying at the Cornwall Inn. I gave Carol a call at the desk, and she said Deborah hadn't checked out yet. She had a reservation through tomorrow. For now, I think things are okay. I don't know who she could possibly talk to that might cause us trouble."

"Her presence in town causes us trouble, Wade. It starts to raise questions. People forgot about Tommy, but knowing he hasn't been seen since then will make people wonder what happened. The sheriff is new. If Deborah pressures him enough, it might make him curious. Hell, Mom might even encourage the sheriff out of some misguided feeling of disappointing Tommy. He might start looking at the old case file and start his own search for him. The farm was the last place he was ever seen. Tell me that won't bring questions into our lap."

"Then we tell him the same story we've always told. Why would we know what happened to him after he ran off?"

"He's dead, Wade. We killed him. Eventually people are going to wonder why he completely disappeared off the face of the earth."

A soft gasp over Brody's shoulder set ice running through his veins. He turned to find Sam standing in the doorway to the bathroom, wrapped in a towel. Her eyes were wide with surprise and fear, her lips parted to speak but silenced by shock.

"I've gotta go, Wade. Call me if you hear anything." He hit the button, ending the call before his brother could respond. Brody dropped the phone to the bed and slowly got up to face her.

Sam watched him warily as he moved, her whole body tense.

He didn't go any closer. She looked like she would spook too easily, and there was nowhere for her to run. She could scream bloody murder on the beach and no one would hear her, but he didn't want her to be afraid of him. Brody hated to see that expression in her eyes. She'd always looked at him with interest and openness, even early on. Now the fortress walls had slammed down. It made his chest ache with disappointment. He couldn't let her slip away over this.

"Sam, I know that sounded bad, but it isn't what you think."

"You didn't kill someone?" Her voice was icy cold.

"No. I didn't kill anyone," he said, and that was true. Heath had been the one to actually kill Tommy, although that was splitting hairs. "Please relax. I'm not some serial killer about to slaughter you in the basement because you've uncovered my horrible secret. I've got enough problems right now without you, of all people, turning on me."

Sam took a deep breath, relaxing slightly but not making a move toward him. "So tell me what's going on, then."

"I can't talk about it." Brody wished he could. He would love to have someone he could confess his darkest secrets to, but the brothers had a rule—protect the family above all else. He sat back down on the bed, defeat hunching his shoulders. "I wish I could."

Sam watched him for a moment before crossing the room and sitting beside him. She wasn't shoulder to shoulder with him like usual, but it was an improvement. "Yes, you can. I know of five million reasons why you can tell me anything you want and know that I would never tell another living soul."

"The confidentiality agreement won't cover this." And even if it did, he didn't want to burden her with it. He'd already dumped enough crap on her this weekend. He looked down at the floor, unable to meet her eyes as he spoke. "You're...important to me, Sam. Even if I knew I could trust you enough to keep this secret, it's only a partial consolation. You'll still know. I don't ever want to tell you something that changes the way you look at me. You're one of the only people in the world that looks at me with something other than shock and disgust. I can't risk losing that."

A hand rested gently against his scarred cheek. He turned to Sam, hoping to see the fear gone. It was. In its place was a drawn brow of concern and a slight frown. He wasn't sure that was much better.

"You won't lose it, Brody. You can trust me with this. I want you to tell me."

Her dark brown eyes were penetrating as she spoke. She meant every word. He had to have faith she meant what she said. Rejecting her promise and walking away without telling her would likely do more damage to their relationship than the truth. He would still speak carefully, though. Some details didn't need to be shared to help her understand his situation.

"Do you remember the first day you came into my office?"

She nodded, a smile faintly curling her lips. "Our first kiss."

Brody was glad that's what she remembered instead of his angry rant. "Before that, when I was so angry… I thought you'd seen my computer and what was on it. It was information on a man, a child really, I knew when I was younger. Tommy. When we were teenagers, we were all living as foster children with the Edens. He was trouble from the start, nothing like the rest of us. I worried about him and what he might do, but the others told me I was just paranoid because of my accident."

"You were right." It was a statement, not a question. She had come to know him so well, so quickly.

Brody nodded. "He did something terrible one day while we were all out working on the farm. Our dad had the flu and was in bed, so we were out there doing our chores alone. Tommy took advantage of that. One of my brothers tried to stop him, and when it was over, Tommy was dead. We were kids. We didn't know what to do."

"Of course not. Most adults wouldn't know what to do, either."

"I was afraid that they would take us away from the Edens if someone found out about what happened. None of us wanted that to happen. It was our home. So we panicked. It was an accident and we should've called the cops, but we were too scared to risk it. We hid the body, cleaned up and pretended like it never happened. When our parents asked where Tommy was, we told them he left in the night. He was treated as a runaway and since he was almost eighteen, they didn't spend much energy looking for him."

"That's a long time for you to carry a secret that big."

"It is. We try not to think about it, but it's hard to forget. I always keep an eye on the internet for people that might look for him. The day you came into my office, I had gotten a report that his sister was searching for him. We'd hoped that everyone would forget. My brother called and told me she's in Cornwall asking questions about him."

"Do you think she will find out the truth?"

"I don't know. Only the five of us kids know the real story, aside from you, and even then, we each only know our piece of what happened that night. We didn't talk about it with each other, much less anyone else. I don't know of any way his sister could find out unless one of us tells her. Or the body turns up."

Sam's eyes widened. "Is that a possibility?"

Brody shrugged. "I hope not. But we were kids, not master criminals. We didn't have a clue how to dispose of a body and keep anyone from ever identifying the remains. We've been lucky so far. Without a body, there's no reason to doubt that he ran away."

"And if someone finds him?"

Brody swallowed hard. "I try not to think about that."

# Eleven

It felt strange to be back in Boston. It was an odd thought for Sam to have considering she was born and raised in Boston and loved it. She had never even entertained the idea of moving, even when her job prospects in town were weak.

She was cold. It was overcast and sleeting. It wouldn't be long before the snow and ice started in earnest and didn't let up until April. The only bright spot in the day was the fuchsia rose that was on her desk again this morning.

Sam looked through her office window and dreaded going out to lunch today. Even to see Amanda. She really just wanted to go back to the island. Everything was different there. Including Brody.

The open, happy, carefree man from the island was gone. He returned to being wary, guarded Brody the moment their jet landed back in Boston. He was still affectionate with her, that hadn't changed, but there was something in his sapphire eyes. A worry. A tension that hadn't followed him to his tropical retreat. She missed that Brody, and she had no idea how to coax that side out of him. At least not at work.

The alarm sounded on her computer, reminding her to go meet Amanda. With another glance out the window, she grabbed her lined, turquoise raincoat, slung her scarf around her neck and grabbed her Coach bag. She paused at Brody's door, knocking gently until he called for her to enter.

"I'm going to meet a friend for lunch at the deli on the corner. Do you want me to bring you a sandwich back?"

Brody nodded, his eyes darting to his monitor several times as she spoke. He was distracted by his work. Another thing she hadn't missed about Boston. He'd barely scrolled through his emails in Puerto Rico.

"That would be great." He scribbled an order on a yellow sticky note and handed it to her. "Thank you."

"I'll be back in about an hour."

Brody gave a quick wave and returned to his computers. With a sigh, Sam shut the door behind her and headed through the various security hoops she needed to get outside. On their island, they hadn't even closed the doors, much less needed fingerprint scans to open them.

She got a text from Amanda as she crossed the street. She had a table in the back of the deli with her food. Sam ordered quickly and joined her, setting her phone on the table beside them.

"You have a tan," Amanda remarked. "I hate you."

Sam smiled sheepishly. She did get a nice tan. And no tan lines at that. It had been indulgent and naughty to sunbathe nude on the beach, but she took the chance while she had it. "Sorry."

"What brought on this impromptu vacation? You didn't mention it the last time we had lunch."

"I didn't know I was going then. My boss wanted to surprise me with a long weekend away. It was spur-of-the-moment."

Amanda's eyes widened. "Wow. This romance is progressing quite nicely."

Sam nodded and opted to take a bite of her sandwich to avoid elaborating. Amanda had no idea of the truth of her statement. But Sam couldn't even tell her best friend that she had feelings for Brody. It was all too fast, and she had to leave so many details of their relationship out of the conversation. Declaring her love for her nameless supervisor would send up a red flag, and she didn't want Amanda to be more concerned than excited for her budding romance.

"Well, while you were cavorting on the beach, I had my own development in the man department."

Sam immediately felt guilty. She should've noticed how much her friend was beaming, but she'd been distracted by her own thoughts. Amanda was wearing one of her nicest outfits, her hair and makeup done with more attention to detail than usual. "What? Do tell."

"His name is Matt. I met him at a bar downtown on Thursday night. They had a band in that I wanted to go see. And since you were out of town, I had to go it alone. Matt was there alone to see the band, too. We started chatting and he bought me a drink. It blossomed from there. We went out Friday night and Saturday night. Then we had breakfast Sunday morning," she added with a sly grin.

"Very nice. Sounds like you two have really hit it off. Tell me more about him."

"He's an investment banker, but he's not stuffy. Thirty-four. He's divorced, but no kids. He's got a really nice place in town. And there's a dragon tattoo on his shoulder that was so damn sexy I almost climaxed the first time I saw it."

Sam and Amanda giggled over her exploits as they ate their lunch. She was glad that her friend had found someone. It had been a long time since Amanda had dated a guy with much promise.

"What are you doing Friday?" Amanda asked.

"I have no idea. Why?"

"Maybe we could all go out. Like a double date. It would be fun. I want to introduce you to Matt, and I'm dying to meet your guy. You haven't even told me his name. What's up with that?"

Sam let Amanda talk, but the moment the first words fell from her lips, she knew the answer. She tried not to feel disappointed about it, but double dating was out of the question. So was going out to a nice dinner at the hot new restaurant in town. Or seeing a movie on opening weekend. Or going to her friend Kelly's annual New Year's Eve party. Sam never had a date for that party, and when it finally looked like she might not be single for New Year's, she knew her date would decline the invitation.

Would Brody even be willing to meet her dad and her brothers? She didn't know. The thoughts had brought down her spirits faster than finding out Brody had committed a crime. Being in love with him on a private island was easy. Loving Brody in Boston, surrounded by six-hundred thousand other people, was another matter.

How exactly did she imagine their relationship to work in the real world? She had no idea.

"Sam?"

She looked up from her sandwich and tried to remember what Amanda had asked her. She opted to ignore the question about Brody's name. "I think he's busy Friday. Maybe another time," she said, knowing full well there wouldn't be another time.

"Okay," Amanda said, looking a touch disappointed. "Let me know when he's available."

"Sure." Sam took a deep breath, relieved that Amanda hadn't pressed the issue. She didn't want to lie to her friend, but it wasn't like there were a hundred Brodys working at ESS. She tried to focus the rest of their conversation on Amanda's romance, which was easy to do. She was all too excited to fill the time talking about Matt.

When they were finished, she ordered Brody's food and headed back to the office. Despite the cold, she took her time walking down the sidewalk to her building. She couldn't make herself move any faster even as the icy sleet pelted her face. The lightness in her heart from the past few days had deflated, and all it took was the suggestion of a double date jabbing it like a sharp pin.

Brody had been an enigma to her. A puzzle she wanted to put together. The more she learned, the more she was determined to learn. Ever the meddler, she not only wanted to know Brody but to help him. He didn't seem very happy locked away in his tower. She had done her best to help where that was concerned. But now what? Had she thought her love would change him? Give him the courage to step into the light?

As she stood dripping onto the rug in the lobby, she realized she simply hadn't thought that far ahead. When

Sam had held Brody's lunch hostage and forced him from his office, she had never expected things to go this far. She never dreamed she would kiss him, much less sleep with him or go away on a romantic vacation. And she certainly never imagined she would fall in love with him.

But now that she had…what was she going to do? If Brody wouldn't live his life in public, was she willing to live her life in the shadows with him?

Sam watched the numbers climb on the elevator as it spirited her up to the top floor. By the time the doors opened, she knew she had her answer. Yes, she would. *If*—and that was a very emphatic *if*—he was happy. And she really didn't think he was happy hiding from the world. Even with her in his life. So now what?

At her desk, Sam slipped out of her coat and hung it on the rack. She didn't even bother to knock on Brody's door. Instead, she slid his lunch through the silver drawer she'd ignored since nearly her first day on the job. Slamming it shut, she slumped into her chair and started reading her new email.

When Brody's door opened and his head peeked around the heavy wood, she immediately felt guilty. His eyes were wary as he watched her from a distance. Apparently thrusting his lunch at him through the drawer after all this time had set off alarm bells in his mind. "Everything okay?"

"Yes," she said, pasting a smile on her face that she hoped looked authentic.

He didn't seem convinced but came out from behind the door. He was looking very handsome today in a gray pinstripe suit and smoky blue tie. Sam still didn't understand why he dressed so nicely when no one would ever see him. She preferred him in jeans and barefoot.

"Lunch go all right?"

"Yes," she repeated, then shook her head. She might as well be honest about how she was feeling. "No, not really. My friend Amanda asked if you and I wanted to double date with her and her new guy on Friday."

His brows shot up. "Your friend knows about me?"

Was that enough to cost her five million? She hoped not. "Not much. Not your name or who you are. She just knows that I've been seeing someone at work. And that I've been very happy."

"You don't look happy," he noted.

"At the moment I'm not."

"Why?"

Sam sighed. "Because you were too distracted by what I might've told Amanda to hear the rest of the sentence. She wants us to go out with her, but we can't. And we can't go out to dinner or a play. Or go Christmas shopping together. *Ever.* Because you don't go out in public."

Brody's face went neutral and stony. If there was a hint of emotion in his eyes over her being upset, he hid it away. "I'm sorry that upsets you. You know that I—"

"I know," she interrupted. "You're the Great and Powerful Oz. The man behind the curtain that no one ever sees. Except me. And it doesn't matter that I see a man who is beautiful both inside and out. That I see a man who is caring and funny. The world will forever be deprived of him."

Brody pursed his lips but didn't respond to the compliments or the complaints. With a sigh, he shook his head and turned back to the subject he was more comfortable with—work. "I have a virtual meeting with the marketing director at one-thirty. Hold my calls until after the meeting is over."

Sam nodded and he went back into his office. She was so frustrated with him, she wanted to shake his shoulders and scream. Not because he was afraid of people's reactions in public. Not because he wasn't willing to do it for her. But because he continued to hide himself away despite how unhappy it made him. That's what really made her crazy.

Those damn scars were a prison all their own. The security measures were a backup plan in case someone was brave enough to try to get close. If Sam could get close enough to Brody's father, she would throttle him with her bare hands for what he had done.

There had to be a way to make Brody more comfortable in his own skin. He'd mentioned how he'd traveled as a teenager to see a specialist about reconstructing his face. That was fifteen years ago. Certainly there had been enough medical advances in the past few years to make a difference. It's not like he needed insurance approval for treatment. He had enough money to do what needed to be done.

She opened an internet window and started searching for skin reconstruction treatments. She scanned through one article after another, site after site. After a few dead ends, she found a fairly promising site for a plastic surgeon in New York City. He was using cutting edge laser technology and other methods. The before and after pictures in his photo gallery were stunning. The results weren't flawless, but they were far better than she had ever imagined. It made her wonder if Brody even knew these kinds of advances had been made in reconstruction technology.

She glanced briefly at the doctor's phone number on the computer screen and a shot of panic rushed through her. Her cell phone. Sam dashed over to her purse and searched through it, but it wasn't there. She checked the pockets of her jacket, but they were empty. She'd left it at the deli. Hopefully it was still there and someone hadn't stolen it.

Sam pressed the intercom button. "I have to run back to the deli. I left my cell phone." She didn't wait for his reply, leaping out of her chair and rushing down to the lobby.

Brody had spent the past hour sitting in his office and feeling like crap. He hadn't said anything to Sam, but he could see the pain and disappointment in her face when they spoke about her friend. She wanted him to be like any other man. To do things most couples did. But that wasn't a possibility. She knew that from the beginning. And yet, she'd hoped for more.

So did he.

He reached out to grab the gift-wrapped box he'd left sitting on the edge of his desk. It was a gold necklace with a sun pendant. The rays of the sun were multiple hues of yellow, white and rose-colored gold. The center was a yellow diamond. Sam was his personal sunshine, and the necklace was the perfect way to thank her for it. He'd ordered it before they left for the trip and Peggy had left it in his home office when he returned.

He'd wanted to give it to Sam several times today, but the timing hadn't been right. He didn't want to give it to her when she was upset. But maybe now was a good time. He could leave it on her desk while she was across the street.

Brody rounded her desk and left the box just to the side of her keyboard. His hand brushed the mouse as he moved away and the screensaver turned off, revealing her web browser.

He felt sick to his stomach when he saw the pictures on her screen. Instead of email or briefing charts, it was page after page of burn reconstruction photos. He clicked back through her search history at a variety of sites, all focused on the latest methods of "fixing" him.

Brody felt the anger of betrayal begin to swirl in his gut. He didn't know why he was so surprised to find this. She was Daddy's Little Fixer, right? She fixed everything else, why wouldn't she want to fix Brody? She'd only played to his ego that night at dinner when she told him she didn't see anything about him that needed fixing.

He was a fool. Stupid for believing that she might be the one woman who would love him just the way he was. Frustrated, he grabbed the pink rose from the vase and crushed the petals in his hand. A thorn stabbed him, muddying his skin with a smear of blood, but he didn't care. It didn't hurt nearly as much as the truth.

A moment later, Sam came through the door with her cell phone in her hand. She stopped in her tracks the moment Brody looked up from her screen. He wasn't sure if it was the expression on his face or her own guilty conscience, but her eyes widened with fear.

"Beautiful inside and *out,* you said. What a load of crap." Brody threw the rose against the wall where it left a wet, bloodstained smear on the wallpaper.

Sam jumped at the violent slam of the flower on the wall, but she didn't move. Or defend herself. How could she? They both knew she was guilty.

"I really thought you were the one. The one woman who could see past my scars and love me anyway. One who would want me for more than my money. I must've been blinded by your beauty. It was hard to see the truth when you were naked and seducing me."

"Hold on right there," she said, sudden anger flushing her cheeks red. "What the hell are you talking about?"

Brody looked down at the screen and read aloud. "'Doctor Jensen's groundbreaking treatments can provide patients with significant improvements to their cosmetic appearance and functional activities of everyday life.' Is that what you want, Sam? You want to fix me so I'll go to your parties and your dinners?"

Her bottom lip quivered as she fought to hold back tears. "Yes, but that's not why I was—"

"You're fired."

"What? Brody, please. It's not what you think."

"I think it is, Sam. I would've given you everything. I would've treated you like a cherished treasure for your entire life. All you had to do was accept me. I thought you had."

"I do accept you! You just don't accept yourself!" Sam slammed her phone down onto her desk. "You are a miserable hermit. You have spent your whole life hiding from the world because you're too afraid to face your fears. I looked on those web pages because I was hoping that one of those doctors might be able to help you. Not because *I* thought you needed fixing, but because *you* do."

Sam's words were like a slap in the face. He nearly flinched from the sting of it. "You're calling me a coward? After everything I've faced in my life you have the nerve to tell me I'm hiding away because I'm scared? There's nothing any person on the street could do to me, Sam, that would be more horrible than what has already been done."

"Then why don't you come outside with me and prove it." Sam marched over to the office door and held it open for him. "Go down into your own damn lobby and say hello to your front desk security for the first time."

How dare she challenge him? Who the hell did she think she was? If he wanted to go to the lobby he would. He didn't want to. And he certainly wasn't going to do it only to prove something to her. She didn't know anything about him. She was his secretary and a temporary one at that. His hands curled into tight fists at his sides.

Finally, he turned away from her. He grabbed her coat, phone and purse and followed her to the door. He threw both of them through the doorway into the elevator lobby, following it with the gift box he'd put on her desk. He didn't want it around to remind him of her. Her purse opened and the contents scattered across the marble floor. "I said you're fired, Miss Davis."

When Sam turned away from him to lunge for her things, he snatched her ID card off of her shirt collar. The door shut as she bent down to scoop up her purse, and she realized too late that now she was trapped. Without her ID, she couldn't come through the door or go down the elevator.

Her face flushed a flaming red as she clutched her coat and purse to her chest. She pounded on the glass with her fist. "You can't just leave me in here!"

Her words were muffled, but he could still hear the angry edge of desperation in her voice. "I won't," he said confidently. "I'll have the head of security come escort you out of the building momentarily."

"And is he going to make your copies? Or bring you your lunch? Or pick up your dry cleaning? Agnes won't be back for another week. You're helpless without an assistant."

"I'd rather have no assistant than have you in this office another minute."

Sam flinched but stood her ground. With a sad shake of her head, she said, "Good luck finding another woman like me."

He nearly snorted with contempt. "Secretaries aren't that hard to come by."

She narrowed her dark eyes at him. "I meant in your bed, Brody. It took over thirty years to get a woman into it. Let me know how long the next one takes!"

That was a low blow and she knew it. She could tell the moment the words crossed her lips and Brody's expression crumbled from angry to just plain hurt. A part of her was glad. She was hurt, too. It was only fair that he feel the same. But then he regrouped and she dreaded what might come next.

"It shouldn't be difficult," he said, his lips curling into an angry sneer. "You aren't the only woman in this town willing to sleep her way to the top. Of course, you must not be very good in bed. Every boss you sleep with fires you."

Brody had gutted her with words. Sam could only stumble back against the wall to brace herself from the impact of his insult. He had reduced their love affair to something sleazy that she'd engineered to further her ambitions and called her a lousy lay in one breath.

There was nothing she could say to that. She closed her eyes and prayed she could keep the tears back a few more seconds. When she opened her eyes, he had turned away. She caught only a second's glimpse of him before he stormed into his office and slammed the door.

The moment he was gone, her bravado crumbled. She slumped back against the wall and slid to the floor. The tears poured out of her almost faster than her body could manufacture them. She could only hold her things to her chest and sob into them.

How had this happened? Why wouldn't he listen to her when she tried to explain herself? She'd sat patiently waiting for him to explain about Tommy's death. She deserved equal consideration for a far lesser crime.

Yes, she wanted Brody to see the doctor in New York. But not for the reasons he claimed. His self-esteem was so low he couldn't even fathom that she would want him the way he was. At the slightest evidence to the contrary, his fears were realized and he pushed her away. Why couldn't he understand that the person who wanted him fixed the most was him?

This morning, she'd been saddened thinking she might never be able to introduce the man she loved to her friends and family. Now, she was heartbroken and none of that mattered because she'd lost the man she loved for good.

Sam looked around, feeling lost. That was when she noticed the box on the floor. It wasn't hers, but he'd tossed it out with her things. She reached for it and opened the box. She gasped when she saw the golden sun necklace inside. It was stunning with a center stone so perfectly cut, it shimmered even in the dim florescent lighting of the lobby.

He'd bought it for her, she realized sadly. What could've been a beautiful moment between them was ruined. She grasped the chain and clutched it against her chest with fresh tears falling.

The chime of the elevator sounded and Charlie, the head of security, stepped out onto the landing. The older man looked at her with concern and then bent down to pick up a tube of lipstick that had rolled across the room when her purse dumped out.

"Come on, Samantha. Let's get you out of here." He held out a strong arm to help her off the ground and slowly walked her back to the elevator.

"I'm sorry about all this, Charlie."

"Don't be. It's the most excitement I've had around here in a while. Despite all the fancy locks and alarms, this isn't exactly like the covert ops I'm used to. I almost never get to walk people out. Especially not pretty young ladies with broken hearts."

How could Charlie see what Brody couldn't? "He wouldn't listen to me. I mean I…I love him. I want him to be happy."

Charlie frowned at her and put a reassuring arm around her shoulder. "I know, kiddo. But have some faith. He'll come around soon. And if he doesn't, Agnes will knock some sense into him the moment she comes back from her trip."

# Twelve

"What, in the name of all that is holy, has happened here while I was away?"

Agnes's sharp words penetrated Brody's near sound-proof walls. He didn't even need to look up at the surveillance cameras to know she was back from her vacation and fit to be tied.

Brody stumbled out of his office to greet her and knew immediately why she was upset. Things had not gone to plan over the past week. Being without an assistant had been harder than he thought. The janitorial staff wasn't allowed on his floor, so he had days of trash piled up outside his door with more than a few stinky food cartons in it. Charlie had graciously picked up his lunch deliveries and brought them upstairs, but that was all the assistance he'd received.

The printer had run out of both toner and paper over the past few days. When he finally found the replacements in the credenza, he'd only had a brief moment of glory before the machine started to jam. The printer was currently in about twenty-three different pieces, scattered across the floor. He'd stayed at work until after midnight, certain he could fix it. Until he realized he couldn't. And he wasn't able to put it back together, either.

He was as big of a mess as the rest of the place. Despite not having a drop of coffee, he hadn't slept more than three hours at a time in the week since Sam left. He hadn't shaved. Instead of his immaculately pressed suits, he was wearing a T-shirt and jeans. It was all he had clean without asking someone to drop off and pick up his dry cleaning. Peggy only handled his everyday clothes, and he'd been too stubborn to ask for help.

Agnes could only stare at him with her arms overflowing with office mail he couldn't pick up. In a huff, she dumped the mail at her feet and planted her hands on her hips. "Brody Eden, is that a bloodstain I see on the wall? What is going on here? What happened to Samantha?"

This was the moment Brody had been dreading. From the second he'd called security and slammed down the phone, he'd regretted every word he said to Sam in anger. He'd lifted weights for nearly an hour to burn off his emotional maelstrom, and when he was calm again, he knew for certain that he was a first-class jerk. Agnes would no doubt confirm his suspicions and not mince words to do it.

"She's...gone."

"Why? Did she quit? I told you to be nice to her, Brody. No one appreciates being barked at all the time."

"No, she didn't quit. I fired her."

Agnes's fingers twitched. He could tell she was itching to grab him by the ear and drag him to a chair where he would spill his guts. He would save her, and his ear, the trouble. "We had a disagreement."

"About?" Her brows rose expectantly. "Don't make me drag every word out of you, Brody. What did you fight about?"

Brody sighed. "She wanted me to go see a doctor in New York that does facial reconstructions. He specializes in burn treatment."

"And this made you angry because…?"

Agnes was going to make him say the words that he dreaded out loud. There was no way around it. If he lied, she would know. "Because I am in love with her, and I thought she was happy with me the way I am."

Agnes's expression softened at his use of the L word. "It sounds as though you two had an eventful month while I was away." She looked around the room with a resigned sigh. "Give me an hour to deal with this mess. I'll go get us some breakfast, stop by the dry cleaner and then we'll sit down and finish this conversation, okay?"

"Okay." Brody was a successful, powerful man, but he knew when to step back and let Agnes run the show. Right now, he'd proven he couldn't do it without her.

"While I'm gone, why don't you clean up in the bathroom, shave and perk yourself up?"

Brody's office had its own bathroom, complete with a shower stall that he used after his workouts. He nodded at Agnes like an obedient child and disappeared into his office. By the time he stepped out of his bathroom, there was a black suit and red dress shirt hanging on the door, still in the bag from the cleaners. Slipping into his usual clothes made him feel more normal and confident again. As did the scent of warm coffee.

The aroma lured him out to Agnes's area. She truly

was a miracle worker. The trash was gone, the mail was sorted and there was a new, fully assembled printer on the credenza.

She was sitting in the guest area that had never actually been used. Brody had put the couch, chairs and coffee table there because the space was big enough and it seemed like the thing to do. But since no one came to this floor, it was more like a museum piece.

On the glass coffee table were two steaming cups of coffee and two breakfast croissants wrapped in deli paper.

Agnes patted the chair beside her. "You're looking much better."

"Thank you for dealing with the mess, Agnes."

She opened a packet of sugar, dumped it into her cup and took a tentative sip. "From the sounds of it, there's still more to clean up. What exactly happened between you and Sam?"

Brody slumped into his seat and reached for the coffee. It was hot, scalding his mouth, but he didn't care. He needed it desperately to think straight. "She's the most amazing woman I've ever met. She is beautiful and stubborn and gentle. She wasn't afraid of me at all. At least, she didn't back down if she was. She looked me in the eye without the slightest hint of revulsion." He shook his head and took another sip. "For some reason she thought I was handsome."

"You *are* handsome, Brody."

"You saying it is like my mom saying it. But I can hardly believe any of you, especially Sam. If it wasn't for the fact that she backed her words with actions, I might never have thought she was serious. She touched me, Agnes. She touched my scars. I didn't know what to think."

"She saw in you what I see. There's a lot more to you than your scars, Brody."

"It all happened so quickly. She kissed me one day. I invited her to my house for dinner, and the next thing I knew, I flew her to *Joya Verde*. Sam was everything I'd hoped for and feared I would never have. I guess I was so afraid to lose her that I pushed her away."

"Did she tell you why she wanted you to see that doctor?"

"She tried to. She said something about wanting me to be happy and accused me of being a miserable hermit. I was too angry to listen at the time. All my brain could process was that I wasn't good enough for her the way I am. Despite everything she said and did, she wanted me to be fixed."

"You know, she might be on to something there." Agnes reached out and took Brody's hand. "You're not happy. And don't tell me that you are. I've worked for you for years, and I can't ever say that I saw you content. You're very successful and comfortable with the way you've structured your life. But what kind of life can you have living all alone?"

"I thought Sam would be enough to make me happy."

"And?"

"She was. To a point. But then I realized that having her in my life only solved part of the problem. She got upset that day because she couldn't introduce me to her friends. I realized later that this relationship was awesome for me but horribly unfair to her. I was asking her to live her life hidden away, but I refused to make even one step toward living my life with her in the open."

"She probably thought that the doctor could help you feel more comfortable with yourself. Sure, maybe she had some selfish reasons for wanting you to be normal, but can you blame her? How many things would she miss out on in her life because you couldn't be there with her? Would you guys elope alone instead of having the big wedding she always dreamed of? Or would she give birth to your children by herself because you wouldn't go to the hospital with her?"

Brody had been so shortsighted. He'd spent so much time alone that he never really considered how his life and his future would play out with someone else in it. Sam had every right to ask more of him, and yet she hadn't. She'd only wanted him to be as confident in himself as she was in him.

"My knee-jerk reaction is to say 'of course not,' but when I really think about it, I know you're right. How did I expect to continue on this way? This life I've lived was okay for me, but I can't subject someone else to it. I know that now. But by the time I put everything together it was too late. I said terrible things to her. I literally threw her out of the office, Agnes. She's never going to forgive me for that."

"Do you think she loves you?"

Brody thought back to the painful tears he'd seen in Sam's eyes as he walked away from her. It looked like her heart was breaking, but he couldn't know for sure. "I'm not certain how she felt. She never told me that she loved me."

"Did you tell her that you were in love with her?"

"No," he admitted. "But I hadn't really figured it out yet. I haven't done this before, Agnes."

The older woman smiled sympathetically. "I know, honey. This kind of thing is never easy, whether it's a first love or your fifth. But you've realized you made a mistake and you love her. So now there's only one question left to ask."

Brody thought he knew what she was going to say, but he let her say it first. He had to figure out what the answer was going to be. It wasn't going to be easy.

"What are you going to do about it?"

Sam was grateful for her new job. Amanda had helped her find a position at Matt's investment firm. She was currently supporting the accounting department. It was a temp-to-hire position, but that was fine with her. She didn't intend to do anything that might jeopardize this job, so she would be a permanent employee before too long. And since her new boss was a plump woman in her fifties who did nothing but talk about her grandchildren, there was no temptation. It was perfect.

Her first day had gone as well as could be expected. She had been worried at first. Not about the job, but about her ability to keep herself together. Normally that wouldn't be a problem, but the past week hadn't been a particularly good one for her.

She had only thought the fallout from the mess with Luke was bad. Sam hadn't loved Luke the way she loved Brody. This time, she couldn't even bear to watch movies on the Hallmark Channel. The big upswept happy endings where the hero did the right thing and won the love of the heroine only made her cry, and not with happy tears. She wanted her own big upswept happy ending. But without a single word from Brody in a week, the odds were that she was out of luck. She wasn't even the leading lady of her own life. From the looks of Amanda and Matt's fast-moving romance, it seemed that Sam was playing the role of the supportive best friend.

The only hiccup in her day so far had been the call

Sam received from Agnes. Her godmother was back in the office. She didn't mention Brody at all but asked how Sam was and what she was doing. Sam was happy to tell her she'd found a new job and the people she worked with were all great. She hoped Agnes would relay the information to Brody so he could stew about it.

Several times as they'd spoken, Sam had wanted to ask about him. But she wouldn't. She really didn't want to know if he was doing fine without her. In her fantasies, he was a mess and she liked it that way. It made her feel better when she lay alone in bed and wished she could see the stars overhead like she could on *Joya Verde*.

Sam's fingers sought out the golden sun pendant at her throat. She should've given the necklace back. Knowing Brody, she guessed it cost more than a year of her salary, but she couldn't make herself do it. It was all she had left of him, and she needed that near to her heart if she was going to make it through this breakup.

"Hey, Sam?"

She turned to find one of the women in the department heading toward her desk. She wasn't certain, but she thought her name was Kristi. "Yes?"

"Do you know where the human resources office is?"

"I think so. I had an in-processing there this morning, so hopefully I can find my way back." It might take her three tries, but she was confident she could do it.

"Great. Could you take this file down to them?"

"Sure." Sam was glad to get up from her desk and move around for a while. If this was going to be her new workplace, she wanted to get familiar with the layout and meet the people. She was always quick to make friends with her coworkers, so hopefully she could fill up her social circle and be too busy to think about Brody.

Luckily, the HR office was right where she left it. She dropped the file off with their assistant and grabbed a bottle of water from the break room before heading back to her desk. She was about to sit back down when something caught her eye and sent the water in her mouth sputtering into her lungs.

There was a bright pink rose on her desk in a silver bud vase.

Sam coughed violently, the water stinging her lungs and drawing pain-filled tears to her eyes. She tried to look around her for the person who had left the rose there, but she could barely see two feet in front of her, much less down the hallway.

When she had finally soothed her lungs and the blood rushed back out of her face, Sam wiped her eyes. The rose was still sitting on her desk. She hadn't imagined it. She walked up to examine it more closely. It was the same vase. She'd left it behind in her hasty departure from ESS.

"You know, the employees that work at the front desk of my building are very nice people."

Sam spun on her heels at the sound of a man's voice behind her. Brody was standing a few feet away, another single fuchsia rose in his hand. She blinked her eyes a few times to make sure she wasn't seeing things.

Brody was still there and looking as handsome as ever in a black suit and a flaming red shirt. But it couldn't be real. Brody didn't go out in public. Ever.

"I feel bad that I didn't meet them sooner. Of course, I gave them quite a shock when I marched through the lobby and introduced myself."

Not only was she seeing things, but her imaginary

Brody was talking crazy. She could not afford to have a nervous breakdown on her first day here. She needed this job too much. Sam squeezed her eyes shut and took a deep breath.

"Aren't you going to say something, Sam?"

At the sound of his voice, she opened one eye and found he was still there. "It's one thing to have delusions. It's another to interact with them."

Her imaginary Brody strode across the room until he was standing right in front of her. She could smell the warm scent of his cologne and feel the heat of his body so close to her. This was a really nice delusion. It was a shame she couldn't have it at home, at night.

And then he touched her. Sam gasped as Brody's palms cupped the back of her upper arms. Her eyes flew open wide, and she found herself gazing into the sapphire depths she'd fantasized about since the first day they met.

She placed one tentative hand on his lapel, then another. "You're really here."

He nodded. "I know. Your new job is so close I was able to walk over here from my office."

Brody walked? Through a public space? "Who are you and what have you done with Brody Eden?"

"I smacked him around until he came to his senses and realized that he was in love with you. And then I knew that I would do anything to hold you again, including walking through several public places to find you."

Sam didn't know what to say. Her jaw dropped open, the words escaping her. There were so many things packed into his last statement she could barely process them. But the word *love* was blinking in her mind like a neon sign.

Brody glanced down at her throat and smiled. "You're wearing the necklace I bought you."

She nodded. "I wanted a piece of you with me. This was all I had left."

"I'm sorry for the things I said to you. I lashed out because you were right about everything. I've been hiding from my life because I was afraid. I punished you because of my own insecurities. Deep down, I could never really believe that you wanted to be with me."

"Why?" she managed.

"Because you are everything I wish I could be and never dared to hope for in a lover. You're confident in yourself. You're comfortable in your own skin. You know your own worth. I envy that about you. I couldn't understand why a woman like that would even look at me twice."

"Brody…"

"But I've realized," he interrupted, "that that's my problem, not yours. I've got an appointment after Thanksgiving with that doctor in New York. I know a lot has changed since I last saw a specialist, but I've been too afraid to go and find out that I'm still a lost cause. We'll see if they can do something to help me feel better about myself. But if not, that's okay, too. I need to learn to accept myself and see value in who I am either way. Like you said at the beach house, I need to find something I like about myself and be more confident in knowing I have good qualities, inside and out. And I think you can help me with that."

So much had happened in the week they were apart. She was stunned by his honest words. "How?"

"First, you can tell me that you love me, because I love you and there's nothing more I want to hear than those words coming from your sweet lips."

Sam's heart was racing double-time in her chest. The blood was rushing to her ears making it difficult to hear anything else. But she heard that he loved her and that was the most important thing. "I do love you, Brody."

He smiled and Sam nearly melted into his arms. He had the most amazing smile. She didn't know how anyone could see any flaws in him when he looked at her that way. He handed her the rose he had in his hand. "This is for you. And so is this."

Brody reached into his pocket and pulled out a small, velvet box. "I told the woman at the jewelry store that I wanted a ring sparkly enough to satisfy a woman with pink glitter running through her veins. This is what she showed me."

He slipped down to one knee in front of Sam and opened up the hinged lid. Inside was the most beautiful ring she'd ever seen in her life. It was a large cushion-cut diamond surrounded by a double circle of bead-set diamonds. The platinum band had diamonds set into it, as well. And he was right. It was sparkly enough even for her.

"Samantha Davis, I was living in the darkness before you came into my life. You're like my own personal ray of sunshine. That's why I bought you that necklace. You make me want to step out into the light and stop being afraid. If you will do me the honor of being my wife, I promise you a wedding with five hundred people there if you want it. I'm done hiding, and I'm ready to start living the rest of my life with you. Will you marry me?"

Sam could only nod yes. The tears flowed over as he removed the ring from the box and slipped it onto her finger. It was the perfect size. Somehow, she was certain he'd found that out on the internet, too. When he stood up, Sam threw her arms around his neck and kissed him.

She was stunned to hear the roar of applause coincide with their kiss. When she finally pulled away and looked around, she was surprised to see they were surrounded by people. Her new boss was clapping enthusiastically with tears in her eyes. At some point, the entire accounting department had come out to watch the proposal unfold. Sam had been so wrapped up in the moment, she hadn't noticed anything but Brody.

"Get out of here," her boss said with a smile. "You're the first assistant I've lost after only six hours."

"I'm sorry," Sam said, although she was unable to hide her grin. She rounded her desk to grab her things, sweeping up her silver bud vase and rose last. Then she slipped her arm through Brody's and walked with him out of the building.

Once they reached the street, they stopped. "Where are we going now?" she asked.

"Anywhere you want."

"I want to go out to lunch."

Brody smiled, but she could tell he was nervous about the prospect. He wasn't going to be comfortable overnight. "Okay. How about that place across the street?"

They headed toward the crosswalk and waited for the light to change. As they passed through the crowd of people, Sam could feel Brody tense beside her. There were some stares, but Sam clung tighter to him and they kept moving. Outside the restaurant, she stopped and turned to him. "Are you okay? Is this too much for your first day out?"

The tension eased from his face as he leaned down and kissed her. "I'll be fine. I can do anything if you're with me. Besides, I've decided that they're not staring at me because of my scars. They're staring because my fiancée is so damn hot."

# Epilogue

*Christmas Eve*

"I don't know what to wear," Sam said from the depths of their closet.

Brody sat on the mattress and shook his head. "It really doesn't matter. We usually wear whatever we feel like. Something warm," he suggested.

"It does matter!" She flipped through several outfits and frowned. "I'm meeting your family for the first time. I want to make the right impression."

"My family has been so concerned about my love life for the past ten years that I think they'll love you on principle. No matter what you wear, they're going to adore the beauty that tamed the beast."

That was sweet, but it didn't make her any less nervous about facing the Edens and their clan of super-successful children. Sam emerged from the closet with

an outfit held up to her chin. It was a plaid wool wrap
skirt and cream sweater that she would pair with tights
and knee-high boots. "What about this?"

"It's great."

She could tell he was humoring her. Sam carried the
outfit back into the closet and came out with another
one. This one was a red sparkly sweater with flowing
black palazzo pants. "What about this?"

"It's great."

She dropped the outfit to her side. "You said that
about the last one."

"They were both great. Really."

Sam sighed. "You're no help at all."

Brody shook his head and got up from the bed to
approach her. He wrapped his arms around her waist
and tugged her close. "You're beautiful in anything. I
actually prefer you in nothing. But you could wear an
ugly reindeer sweater and it wouldn't matter. You're so
fashionable, you'd probably start a new trend of ugly
reindeer sweaters."

He leaned down to kiss her, and Sam felt her nerves
finally start to fade. She melted into him, letting the
latest outfit fall to the floor. Brody's hands glided over
her back. One slipped beneath her top and moved to
unsnap her bra.

"Oh, no you don't," she said, twisting from his grasp
before he could succeed. "We're going to be late getting to your parents' house as it is."

"Then finish packing so we can leave!"

"Fine. The skirt," she decided.

"Fine." Brody smiled, and she realized he'd tricked
her into making a quick decision.

Sam was stuffing the last of her things in a bag when
she heard Brody's cell phone ring. She recognized the

tone now as his brother Xander's—"Hail to the Chief." It always made her laugh when she heard the different songs he chose for each member of his family.

"Hey, Xander," Brody answered. "Are you at the house already?"

There was an extended silence. Sam zipped up her bag and rolled it across the room to where Brody was standing. The expression on his face was not what she was expecting. His face was blank and stony, his eyes boring into the wall. Something was wrong. Hopefully nothing happened with his parents. Brody had told her his foster dad, Ken, had a heart condition.

"Are we certain it's him?" Brody said at last. "So Wade was wrong."

Sam wished she could hear the other half of this conversation. She could only put a reassuring hand on his arm and wait for the call to end.

"I'm not blaming him. I…I had just hoped we had that problem dealt with last year."

She could hear Xander's muffled voice on the phone but couldn't make out the words.

"We'll be there in a couple hours. We were about to leave when you called. Okay. I'll see you shortly."

At that, Brody disconnected the phone and flopped onto the bed. Sam sat down beside him. "What happened? Is everyone okay?"

"For now," Brody said. "Xander says that the local news has reported the discovery of human remains at the site of a new resort being built. On the land my parents used to own."

Sam let his words sink in. "Is it…*him?*"

Brody nodded his head and took her hand in his. "It has to be, although I'm sure it will take the lab quite a while to confirm an identity. I was hoping this day would never come, but I'm pretty certain someone has finally unearthed the body of Tommy Wilder."

* * * * *

*If you loved Brody's story, don't miss a single*
*novel in Andrea Laurence's series,*
THE SECRETS OF EDEN:
*UNDENIABLE DEMANDS*
*Available now from Harlequin Desire!*

*And don't miss Andrea Laurence's next book,*
*BACK IN HER HUSBAND'S BED,*
*Available February 2014*
*Only from Harlequin Desire!*

# COMING NEXT MONTH FROM

# HARLEQUIN®

## *Desire*

### Available November 5, 2013

## #2263 THE SECRET HEIR OF SUNSET RANCH
*The Slades of Sunset Ranch* • by Charlene Sands
Rancher Justin Slade returns from war a hero...and finds out he's a father. But as things with his former fling heat back up, he must keep their child's paternity secret—someone's life depends on it.

## #2264 TO TAME A COWBOY
*Texas Cattleman's Club: The Missing Mogul*
by Jules Bennett
When rodeo star Ryan Grant decides to hang up his spurs and settle down, he resolves to wrangle the heart of his childhood friend. But will she let herself be caught by this untamable cowboy?

## #2265 CLAIMING HIS OWN
*Billionaires and Babies* • by Olivia Gates
Russian tycoon Maksim refuses to become like his abusive father, so he leaves the woman he loves and their son. But now he's returned a changed man...ready to stake his claim.

## #2266 ONE TEXAS NIGHT...
*Lone Star Legacy* • by Sara Orwig
After a forbidden night of passion with his best friend's sister, Jared Weston gets a second chance. But can this risk taker convince the cautious Allison to risk it all on him?

## #2267 EXPECTING A BOLTON BABY
*The Bolton Brothers* • by Sarah M. Anderson
One night with his investor's daughter shouldn't have led to more, but when she announces she's pregnant, real estate mogul Bobby Bolton must decide what's more important—family or money.

## #2268 THE PREGNANCY PLOT
by Paula Roe
AJ wants a baby, and her ex is the perfect donor. But their simple baby plan turns complicated when Matt decides he wants a second chance with the one who got away!

---

**YOU CAN FIND MORE INFORMATION ON UPCOMING HARLEQUIN® TITLES, FREE EXCERPTS AND MORE AT WWW.HARLEQUIN.COM.**

HDCNM1013

# REQUEST YOUR FREE BOOKS!
## 2 FREE NOVELS PLUS 2 FREE GIFTS!

**HARLEQUIN®**

*Desire*

### ALWAYS POWERFUL, PASSIONATE AND PROVOCATIVE

**YES!** Please send me 2 FREE Harlequin Desire® novels and my 2 FREE gifts (gifts are worth about $10). After receiving them, if I don't wish to receive any more books, I can return the shipping statement marked "cancel." If I don't cancel, I will receive 6 brand-new novels every month and be billed just $4.55 per book in the U.S. or $4.99 per book in Canada. That's a savings of at least 13% off the cover price! It's quite a bargain! Shipping and handling is just 50¢ per book in the U.S. and 75¢ per book in Canada.* I understand that accepting the 2 free books and gifts places me under no obligation to buy anything. I can always return a shipment and cancel at any time. Even if I never buy another book, the two free books and gifts are mine to keep forever.

225/326 HDN F4ZC

Name _____ (PLEASE PRINT) _____

Address _____ Apt. # _____

City _____ State/Prov. _____ Zip/Postal Code _____

Signature (if under 18, a parent or guardian must sign) _____

### Mail to the Harlequin® Reader Service:
**IN U.S.A.:** P.O. Box 1867, Buffalo, NY 14240-1867
**IN CANADA:** P.O. Box 609, Fort Erie, Ontario L2A 5X3

**Want to try two free books from another line?**
Call 1-800-873-8635 or visit www.ReaderService.com.

HD13R

SPECIAL EXCERPT FROM

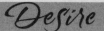

*Harlequin® Desire presents*

THE SECRET HEIR OF SUNSET RANCH,

*part of*

USA TODAY *bestselling author*

*Charlene Sands's*
miniseries

*THE SLADES OF SUNSET RANCH*

*Returning from the front lines, rancher Justin Slade is
about to get the surprise of his life…*

She was a stunner.

He remembered those deep jade eyes, that pouty mouth
and the Marilyn Monroe hair only a few women could pull
off. He would've bet his last dollar that he'd never see her
again. And now here she was…in the flesh.

Maybe he was wrong. Maybe she only looked like the
woman he'd met in New York City that one weekend a year
and a half ago.

Justin removed his Stetson and her eyes flickered.

"B-Brett? Is that really you?" The hope in her voice con-
fused him. "I don't understand. We were told you were killed
in a gun battle."

Silently, he cursed the bet he'd made with Brett Applegate
during a weekend leave in New York before they headed back
to their forward operating base in Afghanistan.

The price of the bet? Reversing roles for the weekend.

They'd emptied the contents of their pockets. Good ole Brett had scooped up all seven hundred-dollar bills Justin had dumped onto the bunk. "Gonna have me some fun being you," he'd said, grinning like a fool.

Justin had blown Brett's meager cash on a bottle of house wine at the hotel, and afterward she'd taken him to her tiny fourth-floor walk-up. He'd been looking for a good time and they'd clicked.

"I'm not Brett Applegate," he told the blonde.

She studied him. "But I remember you. Don't you remember me? I'm Kat Grady."

"I remember you, *sugar*." But he didn't have a clue why Kat was here, looking gorgeous, in front of the Applegate home.

Her eyes softened. "No one else has ever called me that."

Justin winced at her sweet tone. "My name isn't Brett. I'm Justin Slade and I live about twenty miles north of here. Brett and I served together on a tour of duty in the marines."

Her voice dropped off. "You're Justin...*Slade?*"

He nodded.

"*Sunset Ranch* Justin Slade?"

He nodded again. "Maybe we should go inside the house and talk. I'll try to explain."

*But Kat has a bombshell secret of her own.*
*Find out more in*
**THE SECRET HEIR OF SUNSET RANCH**
*Available November 2013 from Harlequin Desire.*

# Desire

ALWAYS POWERFUL, PASSIONATE AND PROVOCATIVE.

*It is only an affair…or so they believe, in this Billionaires and Babies tale from* USA TODAY *bestselling author Olivia Gates*

From their first explosive night, Caliope Sarantos and Russian tycoon Maksim Volkov agreed to no commitment, only pure pleasure. Then her pregnancy changed everything.

**Look for CLAIMING HIS OWN** *next month,*
*from Harlequin Desire!*

**Don't miss other scandalous titles from the**
**Babies and Billionaires miniseries**

## YULETIDE BABY SURPRISE
### by *USA TODAY* bestselling author
### Catherine Mann

## THE NANNY TRAP
### by Cat Schield

## THE BABY DEAL
### by Kat Cantrell

## THE SANTANA HEIR
### by Elizabeth Lane

**All available now from Harlequin Desire!**
**Wherever books and ebooks are sold.**

HD73278